Good Tidings

A MARY O'REILLY PARANORMAL MYSTERY

by

Terri Reid

D0775993

To my family and friends who were always willing to read, listen, edit and, most of all, laugh, and to all those who hear a bump in the night, glimpse a passing shadow or smell the fragrance of yesterday and do not discount it for something ordinary – this book is for you.

GOOD TIDINGS – A MARY O'REILLY
PARANORMAL MYSTERY
by
Terri Reid
Copyright © 2010 by Terri Reid

The author would like to thank all those who have contributed to the creation of this book. Richard Reid, Sarah Reid, Debbie Deutsch, Jan Hinds, Ruth Ann Mulnix, Lynn Jankiewicz and Liz Solomon.

And especially to the wonderful readers who walk with me through Mary and Bradley's adventures and encourage me along the way. Thank you all!

Prologue

Black Friday

The superstore was filled with holiday shoppers who, in the spirit of the season, battled for remaining Black Friday Specials. Patrice Marcum shook her head in amazement as two middle-aged women fought over the last pair of flannel pajama pants marked down to $4.99. As she pushed her cart down an adjacent aisle, she heard the unmistakable sound of a garment being torn in half.

Andy Williams' mellow voice, sounding tinny through the store's PA system, was reminding shoppers that this, indeed, was the most wonderful time of the year. Patrice felt her eyes begin to water again. *Don't think about it,* she ordered herself silently, *concentrate on positive things.*

Her three-month-old son, Jeremy, lying in the baby carrier strapped to the front of the cart, started to stir. She knew it was time to feed him, but if he could only sleep another half-hour, she would be able to finish her shopping and get home. Diapers, milk, bread – the essentials she couldn't do without – were needed.

What in the world was I thinking, attempting to go grocery shopping on Black Friday? She chided herself, *I wasn't thinking.*

So caught up in a blue funk of holiday depression, she hadn't given a thought to the day after Thanksgiving. She initially considered just going to the local convenience store, but the prices of the items on her list were easily doubled there and money was another scarce commodity in her household.

Trying to block out the holiday music and trappings of the season displayed on every end cap, she moved toward the back of the store where diapers and other baby essentials were offered. She didn't want lights, garlands, pumpkin pie mix, cookie sprinkles or the newest Lego gift pack. She just wanted to get out of the store with her meager supplies before her baby woke up.

A small crowd stood waiting for a clerk to bring the second pallet of big screen high-definition televisions out to the middle of the electronics area. A young boy stood by his father, his face wreathed in smiles. "Mom's gonna be surprised, ain't she, Dad?" he said. "A big screen TV is better than a washing machine any day!"

A shadow of a smile flitted over Patrice's face. She glanced at the boy and his father, their eyes sparkling with delight, and sorrow washed over her again. She needed to get out of the store before she lost control.

Adding diapers to the cart, she moved to the front of the store. The cash register lines were ten and twelve carts long.

I'll never get out of here.

She gave a cursory look at all of her choices and finally decided Aisle 12 looked like the best option. No sooner had she pulled into the line than several more shoppers moved in behind her. She was committed to this line now.

"Price check. Aisle 12."

Patrice looked up and saw the cashier holding a pair of flannel pajama pants, scouring it for a ticket.

"They were on sale," the woman insisted. "They are in your flyer."

Patrice recognized her as one of the women struggling over the final sale pair.

The cashier shook her head. "I don't think this was the brand advertised. And since it doesn't have tags on it, I have to check."

"Are you implying I took the tags off?" the woman bellowed.

Patrice silently applauded when the cashier calmly shook her head and politely replied, "Oh, no, of course not, but I have to make sure I charge you the correct price."

The woman snarled. "Well, never mind," she said. "I don't have time to wait for one of your lazy clerks to find their way up here. I don't want those."

The cashier smiled patiently. "Really, it will only be a moment."

"I said I don't want them," the woman yelled. "What, are you deaf as well as incompetent?"

"Merry Christmas," Patrice muttered, feeling her strength and her patience fading away.

Fifteen minutes later, with two more people in front of her, Jeremy woke and decided to let everyone know he was hungry. He started with a whimper. Patrice patted his tummy and spoke softly, "It's okay sweetheart, just a few more minutes and you can eat."

She found his pacifier and placed it in his mouth. He was not happy and let her know by popping it out of his mouth and letting out a resounding wail followed by heartbreaking cries. Patrice pushed the cart back and forth trying to calm him; he just got louder. She placed the pacifier back in his mouth. He choked and then spit it out once again.

She knew everyone was staring at her. But honestly, what was she supposed to do?

Her turn finally came, she loaded her groceries onto the conveyer belt and moved her cart, with the still screaming Jeremy, to the register.

The cashier did not greet her and rushed through the checking and bagging process.

She's probably trying to get me and my screaming baby out of the store as fast as she can, Patrice thought.

She dug into her purse and pulled out her wallet. She opened it to find her debit card was not where it was supposed to be. Patrice panicked and tried to remember the last time she used the card. The cashier folded her arms and waited.

"Just a moment," Patrice apologized. "I've misplaced my debit card."

She placed the wallet on the counter and then emptied the rest of the contents of her purse. No debit card. Her stomach dropped. Finally, remembering the stop for gas, just before they had gone to the store, she dug into her coat pocket and retrieved the card. She smiled up at the cashier, but only received an impatient huff.

Swiping the card, she entered her pin and within moments had her receipt in hand. Pushing her cartload of groceries and screaming baby to the exit doors, she zipped Jeremy's coat and fastened his hat on his head. He screamed even louder.

After pushing her cart through the first set of sliding doors, she looked out the next set of glass doors to see a blizzard in front of her.

The snow was falling so hard she could barely see across the fire lane into the parking lot. Fearless shoppers who had decided to brave the weather found themselves stuck in half-foot tall snow drifts. Several who tried to force their way through the drifts had carts overturning into the snow. Jeremy screamed louder. Patrice was near tears.

"Excuse me; is there someone here to help you?"

Patrice turned and saw an older woman with soft white hair, sparkling blue eyes and a kind smile standing next to her. Patrice shook her head. "No, I'm here by myself," she said, "I mean, just me and Jeremy."

The woman smiled sweetly and peeked over to the screaming baby. "Oh, Jeremy, are you having a bad day?" she asked.

The baby stopped crying for a moment and hiccupped loudly.

"Can you call someone to come and help you?" she asked Patrice. "It really is miserable out there."

Patrice sadly shook her head.

"Well, I know you don't know me from Adam," the woman said, "but I would be very happy to help look after little Jeremy while you get your car."

Doubt and suspicion warred with basic practicality. She really shouldn't bring Jeremy out in that weather. And she couldn't push the cart to the car which was parked at the farthest end of the lot. But the woman was right; she didn't know her from Adam.

"I don't know..." Patrice said. "I really appreciate it, but..."

"But you are a careful mother, and Jeremy is your precious baby," the woman interrupted cheerfully.

Patrice smiled back and nodded.

"I'll tell you what," the woman suggested, "I'll call over one of the store associates and he and I will wait together while you get your car. This way, you will have someone who knows how to watch over babies and someone from the store. Will that be helpful?"

"I don't want to be a bother," Patrice began.

The woman put her hand on Patrice's arm. "Oh, honey, don't be silly," she said. "You're a new mother. You should be taken care of."

Patrice watched the woman walk inside the store and flag down an associate, an older man with an understanding smile. He wore a heavy coat, but because it was unzipped, she could see the regulation blue-colored shirt, khaki pants and identification hanging from his lanyard, displaying "Ron."

"You just take your time getting your car," Ron said. "I'll enjoy having a little break looking after this whippersnapper."

Patrice smiled and this time the tears filling her eyes were ones of gratitude. "Thank you so much," she said, "I really appreciate it."

The woman shook her head. "I should be thanking you," she said. "It's not often I get to look after a sweet baby. My grandchildren are too far away."

"Well, thanks again. I'll be right back," Patrice said.

She grabbed her purse from the cart and slogged through the deepening snow to her minivan. It took her several minutes to get to the van and then several more to clean the snow off the windows. She was so thankful Jeremy was safely inside.

She climbed in the van, pushed defrost on, turned the heat up to high and shifted into reverse. The rush of cars in the parking lot made travel back to the entrance slow.

Patrice pulled up as close as she could to the sliding doors. She hopped out of the driver's seat and jogged over to the entrance. She looked inside the

7

first set of sliding doors and didn't see her cart. Her heart thudded with panic.

She took a deep breath. *Well, of course they're waiting inside where it's warmer,* she chided herself, *stop being such a worry wart.*

She walked inside and looked around. No cart. No Jeremy. She pushed her way to the front of the customer service desk, ignoring the angry comments of those waiting in line.

"I left my baby with one of your store associates while I got my car," she said, "an older man with gray hair. I can't find him or my baby."

The associate behind the customer service desk shook her head. "Did you read his name tag?" she asked.

Patrice bit back the panic. "It was Ron," she said, "I'm sure it was Ron."

The associate picked up the intercom. "Ron to the front desk immediately, Ron to the front desk. Code Adam."

"Code Adam?" Patrice stuttered. "But that's when…"

The associate leaned over the counter. "It's our policy to call Code Adam whenever a child is missing," she said. "Don't worry, everything's probably just fine."

"Hi, Jenna, you called me?"

Patrice turned to see a teenager standing behind her.

"Ron, did you help this lady?" the associate asked.

8

, Patrice grabbed the associate's arm. "No, the man that helped me was older. A grandfather," she cried.

Ron shrugged. "I've been in the back working stock," he said. "Sorry."

"Is there another Ron working here?" Patrice pleaded.

They both shook their heads. "Oh, God, my baby!" Patrice screamed. "They've taken my baby!"

"Code Adam," the associate called into the intercom, "all associates, Code Adam. Baby boy missing from the entrance area."

The associate turned to Patrice. "I'm calling the police."

Chapter One

Mary O'Reilly tried to untangle the garland from the Christmas lights as she perched on the tall ladder in the corner of her office. "Note to self," she muttered, "never store the Christmas decorations quickly with the intention of going back and organizing them later."

The new bell over her office door jingled over the Christmas music playing in the small office, announcing someone's arrival.

"You know, if you organize them before you put them away, it's easier to hang them the following year," Stanley Wagner commented. Stanley was the seventy-year-old owner of Wagner's Office Supplies, the store next door to Mary's office. Even though he was about four decades older than she, he was one of Mary's best friends and a decided tease.

"You think?" Mary replied, continuing to work on an impossible knot.

Stanley chuckled. "I recall that it was last year at about this time I made that same suggestion," he said, rubbing his hand over his chin. "You said you were going to do it in the spring, when things slowed down."

Mary dropped the garlands and lights back into the box on the floor and slowly climbed down the ladder. "No one likes a know-it-all, Stanley," she said. "Besides, I'm a private eye, I like puzzles."

"Oh, so you wouldn't be interested in these extra lights and garland we didn't need next door?" he asked.

Mary turned and saw the large cardboard box in Stanley's arms. "Lights and garland that aren't conjoined?" she asked.

Stanley nodded. "They are actually in their own individual packages, saved from previous years," he said.

Mary shot him a sideways look as she reached for the box. "Is that supposed to be a subtle hint, Stanley?" she asked. "Because it wasn't subtle, and it really wasn't a very good hint."

Stanley laughed. "Want me to give you a hand with these, girlie?" he asked.

Mary placed the box on her desk and opened it. On top of the layers of neatly packaged lights and garland was an obviously fresh bunch of mistletoe – berries and all. Mary lifted it out of the box. "What's this?" she asked.

"Well, no wonder this girl ain't got no beaus, she don't even know what mistletoe is."

Mary shook her head and put it back in the box. "I know what mistletoe is, Stanley," she said. "But this is O'Reilly Investigations. There is no place for mistletoe here."

Stanley grinned. "Why sure there is," he said. "Right over there, above the bathroom door. That way, if you get carried away, you can just scoot inside and close the door behind you."

Mary couldn't help herself; she laughed. "Stanley you are incorrigible."

The door opened and the bell rang once more. Rosie Pettigrew, a successful real estate broker from down the street entered. Rosie's white hair was covered with a stylish red beret which, in turn, was coated with a thick layer of snow.

"Where have you been?" Mary asked. "Alaska?"

Rosie shook her head, snow flying around her. "It's a blizzard out there," she said, "and they're calling for another six inches."

Mary looked out the window and saw a thick blanket of snow covering her black 1965 MGB Roadster. "It wasn't snowing a little while ago," she said.

"How long ago?" Stanley asked.

"Well, I started detangling at about seven-thirty," Mary replied.

"Dearie, it's nearly ten," Rosie said. "And, if you don't mind me saying, if you package up your lights and garlands back in their original packaging when you put them away at the end of the season, they won't be tangled."

Stanley covered his laughter in a cough.

Mary just smiled stiffly. "Thanks, Rosie, that's good to know."

Rosie walked over to the box and peered inside. "Oh, good, mistletoe," she exclaimed, looking around the room. "I think it would work best over the bathroom door. That way..."

"Yes, I know," Mary interrupted. "If I get carried away, I can just scoot inside and close the door."

Rosie looked surprised. "Well, I was going to say it would enhance your decorating scheme with a little green vegetation right in the center of the room," she said, then smiled. "But a little hanky-panky time in the bathroom isn't bad either."

"Good grief," Mary said, her face turning bright red, "can we just get our minds off the hanky-panky?"

Rosie shrugged. "You were the one that brought it up."

Mary took a deep breath. "Let's talk about the weather," she suggested. "So, another six inches by tonight?"

Rosie nodded. "If it falls quickly and then the plows can get in, it will make a lovely setting for the Mistletoe Walk on Sunday."

"Yeah, nothing says 'Happy Holidays' like dirty snow and slush," Stanley grumbled.

The Mistletoe Walk was the annual Downtown Freeport celebration to open the holiday shopping season. It was held on the Sunday after Thanksgiving. All of the downtown businesses decorated their windows to reflect the theme selected by the Walk's committee. Retailers offered store specials to encourage shopping in the downtown area. The Downtown Development Foundation offered horse-drawn sleigh rides, carolers and holiday snacks.

"So, Rosie, is your window done?" Mary asked.

Rosie smiled. "Yes, I'm so excited about the theme this year," she said. "*The Gift of the Magi*, is such a romantic story."

"It's a story about bad communication," Stanley grumbled, "and a waste of money. What are you gonna do with a watch chain and no watch or hair combs and no hair, I ask you? And how the hell are we supposed to decorate store windows with that kind of a theme?"

"I put up a lovely tree with garland that looks like gold chain and ornaments that are hair combs," Rosie said. "It really looks festive."

"Who puts hair combs on a Christmas tree?" Stanley asked. "Maybe Rhonda at the beauty shop, but hair combs ain't gonna sell real estate."

"It's not about selling real estate," Rosie explained. "It's about getting into the spirit of the season."

Mary held up her hand before Stanley could speak. "Just warning you," she said, "if you say 'Bah Humbug,' I'm going to find three ghosts, have them visit you and keep you up all night long."

Ever since Mary had a near death experience, she had been able to communicate with ghosts. It was part of the deal she made when she chose to return to life. Her P.I. work tended to be more centered on those who had already passed beyond than on the living.

"Well," Stanley said. "If you're gonna be mean about it..."

Mary smiled. "You can't fool us, you softie," she said. "I've seen you sneaking Christmas gifts into the back room of your store for months now."

Stanley blushed. "Man can't even do some shopping without every busy-body in town poking their nose in his business."

Rosie giggled. "So, Stanley, what did you get for your sweetie?"

"None of your beeswax," he said, blushing deeper.

"Hmmm," Rosie said, "I did hear a rumor about you visiting the boutique and picking up some pretty fancy lingerie. I didn't believe it until just now."

Stanley stormed to the door. "Damn busy-bodies," he growled.

"Thanks for the decorations, Stanley," Mary called as the bell jingled his departure.

Once he had walked away from the store, Mary and Rosie collapsed into a fit of laughter. "Oh, Rosie," Mary said, wiping her eyes, "that was really mean. We should apologize."

Rosie tapped at her flushed cheeks with a lace handkerchief. "Oh, I'll apologize," she said, with a sweet smile, "next year some time."

She looked back at the box on the desk. "But I didn't mean to chase him off if he was going to help you."

Mary shook her head.

"No, really, not having to untangle the lights is going to speed up my process considerably," she said. "I'll be done by the time the plows clear the street. Besides, I really can't do anything else until they get here."

Rosie looked back out the window and shivered. "Well, I would stay and help you," she said, "but William is driving over with his four-wheel drive pickup and taking me back to his place to wait out the storm. He has a fireplace you know."

Mary grinned and wagged her eyebrows. "William, eh?" she said. "Didn't you go to Rockford with him last week?"

Rosie smiled and sighed. "Yes. Yes, I believe I did," she said, "and he was such a fine gentleman that I decided to let him have the pleasure of my company once again."

Mary smiled and lifted the mistletoe out of the box and handed it to Rosie. "Perhaps you ought to take this with you," she said. "You'll probably get more use out of it."

Rosie grinned, took the bouquet and placed it back in the box. "Some of us don't need mistletoe," she bragged, winking at Mary before she waved goodbye and made her way out into the deepening snow.

"Show-off," Mary called at her departing figure.

She looked at the mistletoe sitting in the box. "You are not going to be hung in this place of business," she growled.

She took it out of the box, laid it on her desk, and then carried the box filled with untangled lights and garland to the ladder. As she climbed up the ladder, a new song began on the radio. Within a moment she recognized it. Frank Sinatra crooned, *"Oh, by gosh, by golly, it's time for mistletoe and holly."*

"Shut up, Frank," she muttered, as she pulled a string of lights out of the box.

Chapter Two

After hanging the first set of lights on her bare wall, she realized that Rosie was right – she needed something more to add to the décor. But that something was not going to be mistletoe. She made a call to Deininger Floral Shop and explained her dilemma. Within a few minutes the downtown floral shop delivered a box of fresh evergreens ready to be hung.

Two hours later Mary climbed down the ladder and surveyed her handiwork. The lights and garlands were now wrapped around long-needled evergreen swags.

She took a deep breath and let the scent of Christmas fill her lungs. There was nothing like the smell of fresh evergreens. The mellow sounds of "Have Yourself A Merry Little Christmas" filled the room and Mary felt a little homesick, even though she had just been with her family in Chicago for Thanksgiving the day before. Accompanied by Kenny G's saxophone she sang along, "Faithful friends who are dear to us, gather near to us once more. Through the years we all will be together, if the fates allow. Hang a shining star upon the highest bough. And have yourself a merry little Christmas now."

The jingling of the doorbell instantly halted Mary's solo and she turned to see her newest visitor.

A young boy, about six years old, stood just inside the door. He shifted awkwardly as he held her gaze and took a deep breath.

"Can I help you?" Mary asked.

He nodded. The sprinkling of freckles across his nose did nothing to lessen his sober expression. "Do you do real people stuff?" he asked. "Not just ghost stuff?"

She motioned to the chair at the other side of her desk, while she sat behind it and pulled out a paper and notepad. "Yes, I work on investigations that involve live people too," she said. "I used to be a police officer."

He settled himself on the chair and met her eyes. "That's good, right?"

She nodded and held back a smile. "Yes, it's good," she said. "My name is Mary O'Reilly. What's your name?"

"Joey," he said. "Joey Marcum. I need you to find my brother."

"He's lost?" she asked.

Joey shook his head. "He got took," he said. "Some bad people took him...today...at the store. My mom's really sad."

"Has she called the police?" Mary asked. "Do they know?"

Joey nodded. "Yeah, they know, but they ain't gonna be able to do much. They said they don't have much information to go on."

"Joey, the Chief of Police is a friend of mine and he's very good at what he does," she said. "I know he'll do his best to find your brother."

"Yeah, probably," Joey said. "But my brother's only three months old and my mom's freaking out. I figured you could help too...then there's more people looking."

Mary nodded. "Okay, Joey, but I'll want to work with the police on this one. Do you have any problems with that?"

Joey paused. "No, I guess you can talk to them."

"That'll be helpful."

"But you can't tell my mom you're working for me," he said, "promise?"

"Yes, I promise."

Joey shrugged. "I don't think she'd understand, seeing that I'm dead, you know."

Chapter Three

Police Chief Bradley Alden tromped through the knee-high snow drifts and made his way across Galena Avenue to Main Street in downtown Freeport. The snow was still coming down with incredible velocity. His small department had already been overwhelmed with calls about fender-benders throughout the city and he knew it was only going to get worse when the sun set and the slush turned to ice on the roads.

He actually wished all he had to deal with were people who forgot how to drive in the snow. That was understandable. But what he could never understand, and what had hit too close to home, was the newest case his department had received.

He shook his head, remembering the distraught and terrified mother whose child had been snatched in the midst of holiday shoppers. Having a wife and unborn baby girl snatched from his life eight years earlier, he understood some of the anguish she was experiencing.

With the help of the local FBI office, the Freeport Police Department had a good description of the kidnappers and had already sent an AMBER alert throughout the tri-state area. The mother had been left in the very capable hands of Family Services. Bradley didn't think he was a coward, but the panic in the mother's eyes triggered his own gut-clenching response and he knew he couldn't remain objective. He needed to pull himself out of the situation and get back to something normal. *Of course*, he thought with a chuckle, *a call from Mary O'Reilly was usually anything but normal.*

Mary.

He ran his hand through his snow-crusted hair. He still didn't quite understand how he felt about her. She was intelligent, courageous, funny, caring and sexy as hell. But she was also slightly loony, stubborn as a mule and claimed she could communicate with ghosts.

To be fair, he had actually been with her to witness two unique "encounters." But he still couldn't wrap his mind around the fact that there were such things as ghosts. The next thing you know, some fat guy in red, driving a flying sleigh, will show up giving out gifts. He shook his head. Maybe he was going nuts along with her.

She had been fairly vague on the phone. Not unusual for Mary. She needed him to come down to her office to meet with a special client. Well, at least he hoped that this time her new client had his head on straight…literally.

The bell over the door jingled as he entered her office. He smiled. Although he enjoyed sneaking up on her, the bell he'd installed a few weeks ago did a good job.

The smells of the holidays met him as soon as he walked through the doors. He glanced around and then smiled at Mary who was seated behind her desk. "Nice job with the decorations."

She smiled back and his stomach tightened a little.

"Thanks," she said. "I think it turned out pretty good."

He unbuttoned his jacket and hung it on the coat rack in the corner of the office. "I hate decorating," he admitted. "Mostly because I'm not good at putting the lights away neatly the year before and I end up with one massive knot of red, green and white."

He shrugged. "I actually end up throwing the whole mess away and buying new ones."

Mary shook her head. "You know," she advised, "if you just take the time to put them in their individual boxes when you take them down, it makes next year's decorating so much easier."

Bradley couldn't quite figure out why there seemed to be a wicked smile hiding behind that statement. "Thanks for the advice," he said, looking around the room again. "Didn't you want me to meet someone?"

Mary nodded and motioned to an additional chair placed on her side of the desk. "Come over here and sit next to me."

Bradley did as requested and once he was seated, Mary took his hand in hers. Instantly he saw the young boy sitting across from them.

"Bradley Alden, this is Joey Marcum, my newest client."

Joey looked skeptical. "Can he see me too?"

Mary nodded. "Yes, as long as we are in contact with each other, he can see you."

"Marcum…I had a call this morning involving a Marcum," Bradley said, his heart clenching. "A child was kidnapped. Was that…?"

Joey interrupted. "No, not me. My baby brother. I've been dead since summer."

Bradley mentally shook himself. He still wasn't used to talking to people who mention dying like other people talk about going to the gym. "That's right," he said. "I remember the child was an infant."

Joey nodded. "Yeah, that's why you need my help," he explained. "So we can get him home for Christmas."

"Joey, I can't promise your brother will be home by Christmas," Bradley explained. "It can take months and sometimes even years to find a missing child, especially an infant."

Joey shook his head. "Yeah, most of the time," he said. "But they ain't got me helping."

"But Joey," Bradley said, "as much as you would like to help, you are only a little boy."

"Not so little," Joey argued. "I was six when I died."

"Still, you're only a six-year-old boy," Bradley replied.

"A six-year-old *ghost*," Mary interjected. "Joey, how can you help us find your brother?"

"I can visit him," he explained. "That was the deal when I died."

24

"The deal?" Bradley asked.

"I was worried because he wasn't gonna have a big brother to protect him, so I talked to God and I got to be his guardian angel."

"What do you mean, visit him?" Mary asked.

"I can go where he is," Joey said. "Then I can tell you stuff."

"Where is he now, Joey?" Mary asked.

"I'll see."

Joey's image faded in front of them.

"How does this kind of thing work?" Bradley asked, turning to Mary.

Mary shrugged. "This is new to me too," she said. "I never knew guardian angels were real."

Bradley smiled. "This from the lady who talks to ghosts."

Mary laughed. "Yeah, weird, huh?"

Bradley shook his head, his smile turning wistful as he studied her face. "Not weird at all," he said. "How was your Thanksgiving?"

"It was loud, messy and I ate so much I thought I was going to explode," she said. "In other words, it was great! I wish you had come along."

He shrugged. "Yeah, it sounds like it was fun," he admitted. "But most of the guys have families and I thought they should be home on Thanksgiving, so...I worked instead."

"You have a family too, Bradley," Mary said. "If you would just..."

Bradley was relieved when their conversation was interrupted by Joey's reappearance. He still wasn't ready to talk to Mary about his missing wife and child. He wasn't ready to ask a "ghost hunter" to go looking for them.

"What did you see?" Mary asked Joey.

"He was in a van and he was crying," Joey said, tears pooling in his eyes. "They were on a highway. The old lady was in the middle seat, sitting next to him, trying to feed him from a bottle. He hates bottles."

"Was there anything else you could see around you? Could you read any of the signs on the highway?" Bradley asked.

"Signs?" he asked.

"Sometimes there are signs showing which road you're driving on," Mary explained.

"And sometimes, if the car has a GPS, they are on the screen too," Bradley added.

She turned to her computer, letting go of Bradley's hand. Joey instantly disappeared. Bradley placed his hand on her shoulder and Joey reappeared to him. Mary turned, surprised at the contact, and then realized what he was doing. "Sorry, forgot," she said.

She Googled "Interstate Road Signs" and found the image she was searching for. She clicked on the familiar red, white and blue badge-shaped sign. "This kind of sign, Joey," she said. "It usually has a number on it…knowing that number would be helpful."

Joey nodded and then faded once again.

Chapter Four

They sat in silence for a moment, then Dean Martin started to croon suggestively, "Baby, It's Cold Outside."

"Stalker music," Bradley said.

"What?" Mary asked, surprised.

Bradley shrugged. "So this guy has this girl trapped in his house and he won't let her leave. Total stalker."

Mary turned and, because of their earlier position, found herself encircled in his arm. Bradley immediately dropped his hand from her shoulder. "Sorry."

Mary didn't even notice.

"He was concerned about her," Mary argued. "He wasn't stalking."

Bradley snorted. "Oh, yeah...concerned. Are you really that naïve?"

"Naïve? I don't think so. I think I'm just not suspicious of innocent gestures."

"Innocent gestures?" he asked. "That song is filled with innuendos."

Mary shook her head. "You're wrong."

Lifting his eyebrows, Bradley stared at her for a moment. Then he shrugged. "Yeah, you're probably right."

Mary smiled. "No probably about it."

Bradley shivered noticeably. "Mary, are you cold?"

Casually lifting his arm, he placed it back behind her shoulder and pulled her closer. "It's pretty chilly outside," he remarked.

Mary found herself pressed up against his warm and solid body. She inhaled a whiff of his scent.

Do they add pheromones to cologne, she wondered silently, *because...well...damn!*

She needed to get out of this cozy arrangement before she did something they would both regret.

"Um, Bradley, I need to finish my decorating."

Did she just imagine it, or did Bradley's arm tighten?

"I saw that bunch of mistletoe on the desk," he said, wriggling his eyebrows suggestively. "I could help you hang it."

What the...? Oh. Duh!

Mary couldn't believe she nearly fell for his ploy.

So, Mary, are you that naïve? Oh, Mary, you're right. Oh, baby, it's cold outside. What a jerk! Well, two can play at this game.

Mary snuggled against Bradley and smiled up at him, batting her eyelashes. "You're right, it is cold in here," she gushed, "and you make it much warmer."

She toyed with the top button of his shirt. "Much warmer."

Bradley's eyes widened for a moment and then narrowed slightly. *So, she thinks she's got me figured out.*

"I could make it even warmer," he whispered seductively. "We could test the mistletoe, to be sure it worked."

"Oh, Bradley," she sighed and turned her head away.

He slowly slid his hand up from her shoulder along the back of her neck and threaded his fingers into her hair. He applied gentle pressure and Mary turned her face to look at him.

Her mother had always warned her that if she crossed her eyes her face would freeze like that – but in this case, she felt the risk was worth it.

Bradley choked. "Mary," he snorted, "you have the most beautiful eyes."

Mary laughed and met his mirth-filled eyes.

The heat hit them both at the same time.

Mary's breath caught and, no matter how loud her inner voice screamed a warning, she couldn't pull away. Her body tensed in anticipation and her heart beat increased.

Bradley felt his heart race. He swallowed and tried to find a reason, any reason, not to bend down and kiss her lips. Unlike Mary's, his inner voice was encouraging him all the way. *Go for it, dude!*

Mary felt his fingers tighten slightly against her neck. His breath feathered against her cheek as his face drew closer to hers.

"It's the number ninety," Joey announced as he suddenly reappeared. "Does that help?"

Mary and Bradley jerked back, like two children caught with their hands in the candy jar.

"That's very helpful," Bradley said, dropping back against his seat. He let his hand slide to Mary's shoulder.

Joey looked carefully at the two adults across the desk. "You weren't going to kiss or something, were you?" he asked. "That's gross. Police guys don't do stuff like that!"

Mary choked and coughed over a laugh.

Bradley ran his other hand over his face, chuckled and pointed to the greenery on the table. "It's because of the mistletoe," he said. "We were testing it."

Joey looked down at the table and then back up at the adults. "That's weird."

"What did you say you found, Joey?" Mary asked, her voice slightly strained.

"Ninety, nine-zero," Joey said. "That's the number on the sign."

Mary nodded, her focus back on the case. "What time did the kidnapping occur?"

"About an hour and a half ago," Bradley supplied.

Mary turned back to her computer.

"What are you doing?" Bradley asked.

"Accessing Google Maps," she replied.

"Look," she said, pointing to the screen. "If they are on Highway 90, and they've been on the road for about an hour and a half – considering the weather – they could either be on their way to Madison or Chicago. But not much further."

"We've got Amber Alerts already in place for both of those vicinities," he replied. "Joey, do you know what kind of van?"

Joey shook his head. "I can only see what's next to Jeremy," he said. "So, I could tell it was a van, but the snow was falling so hard, I couldn't even see the color."

Bradley pulled out his cell phone and called the station. "Hello, Dorothy. I need you to update the Amber alert. Let them know that we have reason to believe that the couple is in a van and are on Interstate 90. We don't know whether they are traveling north or south at this point. Thanks."

"What do we do next?" Joey asked.

"This is great information," Bradley said. "Narrowing down their direction and knowing they are in a van is going to help."

Bradley stood up, his hand remaining on Mary's shoulder. "I'm going to go back to the station and see if I can put it to more use," he said. "Mary, call me if you learn anything else."

Mary nodded.

Bradley leaned over the desk toward Joey. "You are doing a great job being a guardian angel. Jeremy's lucky."

Joey smiled. "Thanks."

The bell jingled as Bradley left the office and Joey grinned. "Every time a bell rings an angel gets its wings."

Mary was astonished. "That's true?"

Joey laughed. "Naw, it was my mom's favorite movie and we had to watch it like a zillion times every Christmas."

Mary laughed for a moment and then turned thoughtful.

"Joey, this is the first time I've worked with a guardian angel," Mary said. "It would help me more if you told me a little about what you can do."

Joey nodded. "I get to be by Jeremy," he said. "Watch over him. Sometimes, I get to interfere, but I can't do that a lot because he has to make his own decisions."

Mary nodded. "So, when do you get to interfere?"

Joey shrugged. "When it feels right," he said. "I get good feelings and I know I can do something."

"And you choose to be a guardian angel?" she asked.

He nodded. "Yeah, just like you got to choose to come back."

She was surprised. "How did you know?"

"Who do you think sent me to you?"

Chapter Five

"O'Reilly, Special Victims Unit, Chicago Police Department," Mary's older brother, Sean, answered the phone.

"Hey, Sean, it's Mary."

She settled back in her chair and watched the snow continue to fall.

"Hey, Mary. What's up? You work off that extra piece of pumpkin pie yet?"

"I still can't believe you forced me to eat that," she responded, a smile playing on her lips.

"Yeah, I forced you by putting it in front of you. Sorry, that one won't hold up in court."

"You did put Cool Whip on it," she countered. "I think that falls under the definition of 'Attractive Nuisance.'"

"Only if you were five years old," he replied.

She sat up and pulled her notepad closer. "Hey, I need your help," she said.

"Sure, what's up?"

She smiled, knowing that she could always count on her family. No questions, no stipulations – just help.

"There was a kidnapping here this morning," she explained. "Three-month-old snatched. The perps were a kindly old woman who volunteered to watch the baby while the mom got her car from the parking lot and a supposed store clerk."

"Yeah, we've seen that MO here in Chicago," he said. "We've actually put up warnings throughout the city and surrounding suburb. Guess they haven't gotten as far as you."

Mary grabbed a pencil from her desktop. "So what have you found so far?" she asked.

"All infants," he replied, "and they are targeting women perceived to be lower-middle class single moms."

"So they don't have the money to pursue them," Mary surmised.

"Yeah, exactly," Sean replied. "We think they're selling the babies. Making it look like a legal adoption, but charging high-end prices for the kids."

"Have you located any of the babies?"

"Yeah, one," Sean said.

Mary could hear the disgust in his voice.

"The couple had a feeling that something wasn't right, so they contacted us," he continued. "The baby was reunited with his mom, but the perps had cleared out and left no traces."

Mary sat back in her chair and looked up at the sparkling Christmas lights nestled within the greenery. "Sean, I've got to find this baby," she said. "What can I do to help?"

There was a moment of silence on the other end of the phone. "Let me think on this for a little while, Mar," he said. "I think we might be able to put together a plan."

Mary nodded. "That would be great."

"Are you okay coming into the city, if I need you?" Sean asked.

She nodded. "Yeah, I can handle it," she said. "It's important."

"Okay, let me fly this up the flag pole and see what we can come up with."

"Thanks, Sean, I really appreciate it."

"Hey, that's what big brothers are for!"

Several hours later, after researching all she could on illegal adoption agencies, she turned and looked out the office window. It was as if she was in the center of a snow globe depicting a small town at Christmas. Light poles wrapped in greenery and lights, garland-festooned street banners displaying "NOEL" in red, green and gold, a few brave shoppers bundled in scarves, coats and knit caps, and fat snowflakes drifting lazily down to the street.

She glanced over to her car and sighed. There had to be at least four inches of snow on top of it and even more surrounding it, a gift from the city's snow plow driver. She grabbed her coat, she might as well get started digging it out. Before she reached the door, her phone rang.

"Mary O'Reilly."

"Mary."

The sound of Bradley's voice on the other end of the line caused her cheeks to burn with embarrassment. *Good grief, what was I thinking?*

"Bradley, what's up?"

Play it cool, O'Reilly.

"I just wanted to see if you were still at your office," he said. "The weather service just issued a new forecast. This stuff isn't going to slow down any time soon. Do you need a ride home?"

Okay, that was sweet. But there is no way I'm getting that close to him today.

"No, I'm fine," she said. "The Roadster does really well in snow."

Well, that was a definite lie.

"Are you sure?"

"Yes, thanks for the offer," she replied. "But really, it'll be a piece of cake."

The Roadster twirled sideways into the driveway, its front fender sliding into a large drift of snow stopping its forward motion. Mary breathed a shaky sigh of relief. It took her a few moments to unclench her hands from the steering wheel and slow the pounding of her heart.

The drive from her downtown office to her home that normally took five minutes required twenty minutes of death-defying, nerve-wracking, hair-graying determination. The Roadster was definitely not made for winter driving.

"Well, that was fun," she exhaled an unsteady breath.

Pushing open the door, she pulled out her purse and computer bag and waited until her legs were steady beneath her. Then she waded through the knee-high snow to her front porch.

The steps looked more like a slalom run than anything resembling stairs, so she slipped her purse and computer bag over her shoulder, grabbed onto the rail with both hands and slowly pulled herself up to the porch.

"Hi, Miss O'Reilly. Do you want me to shovel your snow for you?"

Mary turned to see ten-year-old Andy Brennan, one of the youngest of the seven Brennan children, who lived in the big house on the corner. He was dressed in a multi-colored collection of hand-me-downs, a bright blue wool hat, red gloves, a brown coat and black boots. *At least he has brothers, not just sisters, who are older than him*, Mary thought, remembering some of the hand-me-downs she received from her older and much bigger brothers.

"How much are you going to charge me?" she called back to him.

He sighed. His normally mischievous face subdued. "Mom says I'm supposed to do service, seeing that this is a snowstorm and all," he explained, "so I'm not charging at all."

"Well, that presents a big problem for me," Mary replied.

"Why?"

"Because I've set aside twenty dollars for someone to shovel my walk, my porch and my driveway," she replied. "And if I don't pay them, it will mess up my budget." She shook her head and grimaced. "I don't do accounting very well."

Andy grinned, exposing a lovely gap where his front tooth used to be.

"What happened to your tooth?" she asked.

Andy's grin got bigger. "David thought it would be cool to have a missing tooth for Christmas, so we could sing that song. So he helped me pull it out."

Ouch, Mary winced.

"It wasn't too bad," he explained. "We used the taffy apple method. I bite into a Taffy Apple real hard and David pulls it out of my mouth." His eyes gleamed with pride. "It only took three Taffy Apples."

Mary laughed. "Good for you," she said, "that was brilliant."

Andy shook his head. "That ain't exactly what Mom said."

Mary was delighted. "Well, she can't say that, because she's a mom."

Andy nodded. "Yeah, that's kind of what I figured too."

"So, do we have a deal?" Mary asked.

Andy nodded. "I'll have everything shoveled in a flash."

"That sounds great," Mary said. "Just knock on the door when you're done."

"Okay, I will."

Mary trudged through the snow on her porch and pulled her door open. The warmth of her room greeted her. "Nice," she purred, and dropped her purse and computer bag on the desk next to the door.

An hour later, Andy knocked on the door. Mary answered the door wearing jeans, an oversized flannel shirt and thick wool socks. Mary peered over his shoulder to inspect the job.

"Wow," she exclaimed. "That looks great. You even shoveled around the Roadster."

Andy nodded. "You must be the best driver in the world," he said, "'cause I ain't never seen anyone be able to park like that."

Mary grinned. "It takes years of professional training," she said. "Most people shouldn't even try to attempt it."

Andy laughed. "You're lying, right?"

Mary nodded. "I sure am."

She handed him an envelope and a paper sack. "The envelope has our agreed to price," she said. "Thank you for not messing up my budget. And the sack has a dozen brownies from Coles Bakery. I bought them in a moment of weakness; you just saved me from making a pig of myself."

"I'll give my mom the brownies before I tell her about the money, okay?" Andy asked. "Chocolate always makes her happier."

Mary nodded. "You are a very wise young man."

Then a thought came to Mary.

"Andy, did you know a boy named Joey Marcum?"

Andy nodded. "Yeah, he was in first grade at my school," he said. "He died in the summer."

"Do you know how he died?"

"He and his dad were in a car accident," he explained. "It was when the flood happened. The bridge got washed away, but his dad didn't know, so his car got caught in the water. Joey died and his dad is still in the hospital."

"That's so sad," Mary said.

"Yeah, Mom says we never know when our last day on earth could be, so we should be nice every day."

Mary nodded. "Your mother is very smart."

Andy shrugged. "Yes, I guess so, but she has to be, she's a mom."

"My mom is exactly the same way," Mary confessed. "It's often scary."

Andy nodded, his face serious. "Can your mom tell what you've been thinking, too?"

Mary bit back a grin and nodded seriously. "Yes, she can," she replied. "I think she has x-ray vision."

Andy agreed. "Dad says we don't stand a chance."

Mary rubbed his head and grinned. "No, we don't," she said. "Now get home before you're late for dinner and you get us both in trouble."

"Not if I have brownies," Andy called, holding up the bag as he tromped down the stairs. "Bye, Miss O'Reilly."

"Bye, Andy," she called, "thank you."

She closed the door with a smile on her face. *Sometimes it's good to remember what life is really about.*

Chapter Six

Mary sat up in her bed. The moon reflecting against the snow shone through the windows, casting a soft glow across the room. She looked over at her digital clock-radio, it read three o'clock. *The witching hour*, she thought.

She tossed aside her blankets, slipped out of bed, walked to the door and waited for a moment, listening to the sounds of her house.

Although Mary had gotten use to nocturnal visitors from beyond the grave traipsing through her home in the middle of the night, ever since a serial-killer had invaded her home last month, she was more wary. *I ought to get a cat*, she thought, *and then I can blame all weird sounds on him.*

She could hear rustling around in the kitchen. Drawers and cabinets were being opened and closed rapidly, as if someone were searching for something. *Not very stealthy for a serial-killer,* she decided.

She slowly crept down the stairs, peering around the corner before entering the room. A tall, slim, shadowed figure on the other side of her kitchen counter was moving systematically through the room. Silently entering, she watched him for a few moments. He was manic in his actions, opening a cabinet or drawer, glancing inside, closing it and moving on to the next.

Closer now, she could see that he was dressed in ragged Army fatigues that were spattered with mud and traces of blood. His tiger-striped Boonie Hat, reminiscent of the Vietnam War, drooped sideways covering her view of most of his face. She could, however, see traces of mud brown camouflage face paint.

"Can I help you find something?" she asked.

He turned and she saw the place where the bullet had entered his forehead. She was grateful the hat was hiding the exit wound.

"I have to find the letter," he whispered urgently. "I should have told her. But I thought I'd have time." He turned back to the cabinets and started opening them.

"Where did you put the letter?" Mary asked.

He turned back to her, a look of confusion on his face. "I can't remember," he said. "It was in my stuff. What happened to my stuff?"

She could see the tattered name tag on the right shirt pocket of his fatigues, "Kenney," and she could tell by the insignia on his shoulder that he was a Private.

"Private Kenney," she said.

"Yes, ma'am," his reply was immediate.

"When did you die?"

It took him a moment to respond. His eyes glistened with tears and he wiped them away with the back of his sunburned hand. "On my twenty-first birthday, ma'am," he answered and then he faded away.

Chapter Seven

"Mary! Mary!"

The incessant voice slipped into her sleeping subconscious and she tried to ignore it.

"Mary! Mary, are you sleeping?"

The image of a six-year-old ghost connected in her memory with the voice and she opened her eyes. "Joey, what's wrong?"

"You have to get up so we can go get Jeremy," he said.

"Do you know where they are?" she asked, glancing over to the clock. Five a.m. *Don't ghosts ever sleep?*

"They brought him to a really tall apartment," he said. "That will be easy to find."

Mary shook her head. "In Freeport that would be easy to find," she explained, knowing there was only one building in town over ten stories. "But in Chicago or Madison or any other big city, there are hundreds of tall apartment buildings."

Joey sighed. "I thought I was helping."

Mary sat up in her bed and leaned back against the headboard. She smiled at Joey. "You are being helpful. Now we know that he's in an apartment, not a house," she said. "All we have to do is pin down some details."

"So what do we do next?"

"I have a big brother," she answered. "He looks out for me, just like you look out for Jeremy. He's also a policeman in Chicago, a special one that tries to find missing people. He's going to call me today so we can work out a plan to find Jeremy."

Joey grinned. "Really?"

Mary nodded. "Really. But we'll need your help to find him. Did you look out the apartment window? Did you see anything that could help us?"

He shook his head. "Just lots of snow," he replied.

The snowstorm had dumped at least ten inches all over the tri-state area. Mary wasn't surprised with Joey's description. Unfortunately, that information was not going to bring them any closer to Jeremy's location. Mary had another idea.

"Can you listen to the man and woman talking?" she asked. "Could you spy on them and tell me what they are saying?"

Joey nodded. "Yeah, I can listen. I can spy. I can do that really well."

"Great! While I wait for my brother to call, you spy on them and give me any information that you think is helpful."

"Okay," he said with a smile. "Thanks, Mary!"

Once he faded away, Mary thought about going back to sleep, but her mind was racing with ideas. *I hate when that happens*, she thought, as she climbed out of bed.

Fifteen minutes later, she was comfortably dressed in an oversized sweatshirt, baggy sweatpants and thick wool socks. Freeport was snowed under and no one was going anywhere. She made a mug of her gourmet hot chocolate, threw some logs into the fireplace and then moved her laptop to the coffee table, so she could work in front of the blazing fire.

After searching through the local Vietnow website, she was able to find some basic information about her nighttime visitor. Private Patrick Thomas Kenney was born on December 24, 1947 and had died, as he had mentioned the night before, on his birthday, December 24, 1968. He was in the 101st Airborne Division and had died in Quang Nam on his twenty-first birthday.

Mary sighed and blinked away the tears that filled her eyes. Although his death occurred more than forty years ago, she was certain there were still family members who remembered a lost son every year at Christmas time and mourned for him.

The phone rang and Mary jumped. "O'Reilly."

"Hey, how are you doing this morning?" Bradley asked. "How was your drive home?"

From her seat on the floor, she could glance out the window and just see her car positioned horizontally across the driveway. "Pretty uneventful," she lied.

Bradley chuckled. "So you parked like that on purpose?"

She jumped up and went to the window. Bradley's cruiser was at the curb. "Is this police harassment?" she asked.

"No, I called to inform you that today is 'Make Breakfast for your Favorite Cop Day,'" he responded, "your favorite cop who has been up all night dealing with the damn snowstorm."

Mary chuckled. "Wow, I didn't realize," she said. "But there's no way I can make breakfast for my favorite cop today."

"Why not?"

"Because my dad's in Chicago," she said. "There's no way I could drive there in time for breakfast." She sighed heavily. "So I suppose I'll have to settle," she said. "Would you like some breakfast?"

Mary watched him hop out of the cruiser and make his way through the newly fallen snow to her porch.

"Well, since you asked," he said into the phone, just before rapping on the door.

Laughing, she opened it as she hung up the phone.

Bradley pounded his snow-covered boots on the welcome mat just inside the house, and then slipped them and his coat off. "Have you heard anything from Joey?" he asked.

Mary took his coat and hung it over a chair near the fireplace. "Yes, he dropped in this morning at five," she said. "They have Jeremy in an apartment

46

building. Joey's back there listening to any conversations he thinks might be helpful."

Bradley nodded, following her into the kitchen. "That's a good idea," he said. "Did you contact your brother?"

Mary poured Bradley a mug of hot chocolate and set it before him on the counter. "What? No whipped cream or marshmallows?" he asked.

She grinned, pulling the container of aerosol whipped cream out of the refrigerator and topping the beverage with several inches of frothy sugar. "You are such a whiner."

He laughed, took a sip and licked away the excess whipped cream.

"So...my brother," she said. "I called him and he was familiar with their MO. They had actually sent bulletins out to the closer suburbs warning shoppers."

"And that's why they came to Freeport," he added.

Mary nodded. "Yeah, far enough to be anonymous and close enough to get back home within a couple of hours."

She took a cast-iron frying pan from a shelf and put it on the stove. "Bacon and eggs?"

Bradley smiled. "I will be your slave for life."

"Does that mean no parking tickets for life?"

"The way you park? Hell no. We earn half of our annual budget on your tickets alone."

She glared at him and began to put the frying pan back on the shelf. "I meant, cold, stale cereal good for you this morning? I think I have something with bran."

"Okay, who needs a budget anyway," he said.

She put the pan back on the stovetop. "I thought you'd see it my way."

"Bribing an officer of the law?" he asked.

"On my salary, no way," she grinned.

He took another sip of chocolate. "Why did you decide to leave Chicago and come to Freeport?" he asked. "You had a stellar reputation there. You could have worked as a consultant for them and made real money."

Mary pulled the eggs, bacon and butter from the refrigerator and placed them on the counter. "Were you ever in charge of a big day-long event where people called your name constantly?" she asked. "Then, when you finally got home, you could still hear them calling you, even in your sleep?"

Bradley nodded. "Yeah, I've had those kinds of days."

"Well, that's kind of what it's like for me to go into Chicago," she explained. "There are thousands of spirits there who have unfinished business and they are all drawn to me. It's overwhelming."

Bradley leaned forward on the counter. "So, how does it happen? You step into the city and you're attacked?"

"No," she said, taking a moment to gather her thoughts. "Ghosts still 'live' in the same time period as their deaths."

Bradley nodded. "That's why you ran into the Apple River Fort last month, because it hadn't been built yet when the little girl you were following died."

She smiled. "Yes, exactly. And from what I've learned so far, every ghost makes his own unique path or journey. Some are daily journeys, which is why so many people see a ghost at a certain time every night. They catch the ghost at that point in their journey."

"But some journeys are longer?" he asked.

Mary laid several strips of bacon in the pan, while she considered his question.

"Yes, some journeys can even be year-long," she explained. "Like Indian tribes, they lived in certain areas during certain times of the year. Some people tell me their houses only seem haunted in the fall, for instance. That's because the ghost's journey is taking them there for that season."

"Wow, snow-bird ghosts," Bradley said, shaking his head.

Mary laughed. "Yeah, sort of. But that doesn't always happen. When people are killed suddenly or tragically, often their ghost is confused and they stay bound to that area until someone can help them."

"Someone means you," he said.

She nodded. "I don't think there's many of me around," she said with a shrug. "Which is why, once they realize I can see them, they get excited and rush over."

"So, can this excitement be dangerous to you?"

She shrugged. "I suppose it could," she said, "like a spiritual stampede. But I've made sure I take precautions when I go home."

"What kind of precautions?"

"Well, I make sure I have sage, which is an energy cleanser, in my car when I drive," she said. "I learned to do that after I was driving down Lake Shore Drive and found John Dillinger in the passenger's seat."

"But Dillinger was supposedly gunned down in 1934," he said.

"Yeah, he wasn't too happy about that," she replied, flipping the bacon over. "And he wasn't thrilled when I nearly drove us into the lake because he surprised me. He made some derogatory comment about women drivers. Did you know that John Dillinger was sexist?"

"No, I didn't," Bradley replied, fascinated with the whole conversation.

Mary nodded. "Yeah, but when I explained that I wasn't in a position to help him because I was just learning the ropes, he took it pretty well," she said.

She scooped the bacon out of the pan and cracked the eggs into it.

"Then we put holy salt around the entrances and windows at my parents' house," she said. "It keeps the spirits out."

"You had spirits visiting your parents?"

Mary nodded. "Yes, and they weren't all nice polite spirits like Joey," she explained. "Some actually threw things to get my attention."

She chuckled. "Of course, that finally convinced my brothers I hadn't lost my mind and I could actually see ghosts. So it wasn't all bad."

"So, if you could take precautions and learn to deal with things, why didn't you stay?"

Mary shook her head. "Oh, I can deal enough to go into Chicago and visit, like I did for Thanksgiving," she said. "But once I stay someplace for a period of time, they are drawn to me. Hundreds, no thousands, of ghosts. There is no way I can protect myself from something like that. So, I live here and visit there."

She put a plate of food down in front of Bradley. He smiled, lifted a piece of bacon and bit into it. "Well, I for one am really glad you did."

She smiled back. "Thanks, I'm glad too."

Chapter Eight

Joey reappeared just as Bradley was finishing his second cup of hot chocolate. "They're yelling at each other," he said in a rush. "They're yelling real bad."

Mary slipped around the counter and placed her hand on Bradley's shoulder. "Joey," she said to Bradley and he nodded in understanding.

"What where they yelling about?" she asked.

"It was about a bird," he said. "Someone must have let their bird loose because he was yelling that the pigeon was gone."

"What else did they say about the pigeon?" Bradley asked.

"That the pigeon got cold feet, which makes sense 'cause it's snowing outside," he reasoned. "And they were in lots of trouble because they needed to dump the merchandise fast because it was getting too hot."

Bradley and Mary exchanged glances. "I'm calling Sean," she said.

She put her phone on speaker and dialed the number.

"O'Reilly," the deep male voice answered.

"Hi, Sean, it's Mary," she replied. "I have an update about the kidnapping case. Joey, the brother of the infant who was kidnapped, is my client. He is a ghost and the victim's guardian angel."

"Okay," Sean said. "I think I've got that, Mary. How old is Joey?"

"He's six," Mary said, "and he's been with Jeremy listening to the couple who snatched him. He just reported the couple who took Jeremy is fighting because their pigeon got cold feet."

"Well, that changes the dynamics," he said.

"Sean, this is Chief Alden, Freeport Police Department. What do you anticipate with this change?"

"Hey, I heard about you. Nice to meet you," Sean replied. "Good question. The perps are anxious and feel we are getting close. So, they will either look for a quick drop or... Is Joey still there?"

"Yes," Mary said, "he's listening."

"Okay, well, they might look at other ways to quickly relieve themselves of the problem."

"Does he mean they're going to kill my brother?" Joey demanded.

Mary took a deep breath. "That's a possibility, Joey," she said, "but in Chicago there is a law that you can drop a baby off at a hospital or fire station or police department, and they won't stop you or ask you any questions. So there is a good chance they will do that."

"Sorry, Joey," Sean said. "What we have to do is give them another option." He paused for a moment. "Hey, Joey, Mary said you can be there with your brother. Any chance you saw the phone number the call came from?"

Joey's eyes lightened. "They wrote it down. They didn't answer the phone right away. They wanted to call them back with another phone. I'll be right back."

Joey disappeared.

"What did he say?" Sean asked.

"They wrote the number down, he's going to check it out," Mary said.

"He's gone then?" Sean asked.

"Yes," Mary replied.

"Okay, I'll make this quick. There is no way they are going to risk being caught by dropping the baby someplace safe," Sean said. "They've done it before. We found the baby in a dumpster and in this weather…"

"Okay, what do we do?" Bradley asked.

"You've always wanted a kid, right Mary?" Sean asked with a chuckle. "I'm going to give you a chance."

"Okay, I'm in," she said.

"Once we get the number from Joey, I want you to drive in," he said. "I can clear you easily for undercover. Then we get things going. It's got to be quick, Mary, or the kid is dead."

Bradley turned to her. "But what about…?"

Mary shook her head to silence him. "Okay, Sean, I'll call you as soon as Joey gets back. I'll meet you at the folk's place by noon. How does that sound?"

"Great, I'll meet you there and find a husband for you," he said.

"Just as long as it's not Coroner Wojchichowski's nephew," she added. "He might want to make it a permanent arrangement."

Sean laughed. "Yeah, I'll be sure it's some cute young beefcake from Vice. I understand the Vice guys are the hot ones."

Mary chuckled. "You were in Vice, weren't you Sean?"

"Like I said, Mary, the hot ones."

Mary hung up the phone and Bradley's hand caught her shoulder and turned her to face him. "How dangerous is it going to be for you? The truth?"

Mary shrugged. "It all depends on how long I'm there and where I stay," she said.

"I'm driving you in," he said.

"No, Bradley, really, I'll be fine."

"I'm driving you in," he repeated.

"Now you're moving from sweet to annoying," she said. "Don't be annoying, Bradley."

"Mary, look out the window at your car," he countered. "The Roadster might be stuck in that position until the spring thaw."

"I got it in there, I can get it out," she said. "Besides, other people were impressed with my driving ability."

"Who?"

"Someone," Mary evaded, "a young man I know."

"Who? Andy Brennan down the street?"

55

"How did you...?" she began. "I mean...no."

"Busted. I'm driving you in," he paused and lifted his hand to stop her from immediately commenting. "Not because I think you are incapable of driving yourself. But because this is my case too, and I want to know what's going on. Think of it this way, now you won't have to worry about a ghost passenger catching a ride and distracting you. Besides, you're my friend and I want to help."

"Damn it, Bradley, you had to be sweet at the end, didn't you?"

"So, I'm driving?" he asked.

She sighed and nodded. "Yes, you're driving."

Chapter Nine

Bradley was sorting through the paperwork on his desk, clearing things up before his trip to Chicago, when the phone rang. "Chief Alden," he said.

"Alden, this is Christa at the warden's office at Dixon Correctional Facility calling with a courtesy call to inform you that Anthony Scarlett was released today," she said.

Bradley ran his hand through his hair. "Thanks, I appreciate the call," he said. "Can I get a copy of his exit interview?"

"Sure, we'll e-mail it to you as soon as it's transcribed," she replied. "He still talks about you. Still says you set him up."

"Yeah," Bradley said. "I put the gun in his hand, put the money in his car, put the drugs in his body and shot the bank guard. I'm just sneaky that way."

Christa chuckled. "Well, keep an eye open, just in case," she said.

"Thanks, I appreciate it."

Bradley hung up the phone and shook his head. *Just what I need, an ex-con gunning for me.*

Mary searched through her closet, picking out the items she wanted to bring to Chicago when Joey came back.

"Where are you going?" he asked.

Mary turned with a start. "Joey, you scared me."

Joey grinned. "Duh. I'm a ghost."

Mary laughed. "Okay, you've got me on that one. Did you get the number?'

"Yeah, they threw it away, so I had to search the garbage, but I have it. It's 312-555-4809."

Mary jotted down the number. "It's a Chicago number, so we can presume they brought Jeremy there. This is really going to help us find your brother. As soon as I send this on to Sean, I'm going into Chicago and help find Jeremy."

"I know you'll find him," Joey said, trust shining in his eyes. "You're lots smarter than those bad guys."

Mary bent down next to Joey. "I'm going to do everything I can to find Jeremy," she said. "But I'm not sure how it works with you and me communicating once I get there."

Joey smiled. "Oh, don't worry. Now that we're friends, I can follow you wherever you go."

"Even in places that have protection, like holy salt?" she asked.

Joey nodded. "Yeah, 'cause I'm a guardian angel, things like that don't bother me."

"Great! I'll call Sean and get him going on this phone number."

"Okay, I'll go back and watch over Jeremy. And if they take him out of the house, I'll let you know right away."

Mary nodded. "That's wonderful, Joey. Jeremy is lucky to have a big brother like you."

Joey smiled. "Guess it's a good thing I died, huh?"

Mary's heart tightened a little. "I guess God knows what He's doing."

Joey nodded and faded away.

After relaying the information to Sean, Mary called Rosie and Stanley to see if they could make it to her house. Less than twenty minutes later both of her friends were seated at her table taking notes and drinking tea.

"So, the only thing you know about Private Kenney is his name, birth date and death date?" Stanley asked.

"Well, his home town is Freeport, so he grew up here," Mary responded.

"And he was looking for a letter?" Rosie asked. "Do you know what the letter is about?"

"No, I only got a few moments with him," she said. "But it seemed the letter was very important to him. It might be what he needs to move on."

"Well, we can check the old high school yearbooks and see if we know anyone who remembers him," Stanley suggested.

Rosie nodded. "I seem to recall a Kenney who used to have her hair done when I had my shop. If I remember correctly she was a Clairol, number ten, ash blonde."

"That will certainly be helpful," Stanley added. "Now if you can only remember the shade of her toenail polish, we should have this mystery solved."

Rosie turned to Stanley. "You're just jealous because I can remember things past what I had for breakfast this morning."

"Well, what I had for breakfast is probably a whole lot more important than someone's hair color forty years ago," he replied.

"Not if I have her name and address on an index card that's sorted according to hair color," Rosie snapped back.

She paused and with a look of astonishment turned to Mary. "I have her name and address on an index card," she said. "I could contact her."

"Rosie, that is wonderful," Mary said. "But before we start contacting people, let's find out all we can about this ghost. We don't want to open old wounds if we don't have too."

"So, Mary, you still haven't told us where you're going," Stanley said.

"I'm going into Chicago to work on a new case."

"Um, dear, you're not driving on your own, are you?" Rosie inquired hesitantly.

"Why is everyone criticizing my driving?" she asked.

"Have you looked in your driveway lately?" Stanley asked.

Mary rolled her eyes. "It was snowing; it was icy," she said. "The Roadster isn't built for those kinds of conditions."

Stanley nodded. "I can see that."

"Funny, Stanley, you sound like Bradley."

Both of their ears perked.

"Bradley, as in Police Chief Alden?" Rosie asked.

Mary, not aware of the undercurrent at the table, responded blithely, "Yes, he insisted on driving."

Stanley and Rosie exchanged delighted glances.

"He's going into Chicago with you?" Stanley asked. "For several nights?"

Mary, reviewing her checklist, nodded absently. Rosie stood, walked around the table and hugged Mary. "Oh, I knew it would finally happen," she gushed. "I am so happy for you!"

Mary shook her head. "What happened?"

"You both finally wised up and took advantage of the situation," Stanley said.

"What are you two talking about?"

"You and Bradley...together...in Chicago... for a couple of days," Rosie said, raising her eyebrows with emphasis after each comment.

"Bradley and I...solving a kidnapping...with my brother...and another police officer pretending to be my husband," Mary responded with mock emphasis.

Stanley snorted. "Nothing but fools," he muttered. "Plain as the nose on my face. Don't see an opportunity when it presents itself."

Mary laughed and gave each of them a hug. "Will you stop matchmaking?" she said. "Really, it's not going to work."

A quick knock sounded on the door.

"That's Bradley," Mary said. "Are you both certain you want to help?"

"Well, it's obvious you need help," Stanley grumbled, picking up his coat and notebook. "No problem, missy, no problem at all. Just watch yourself in that big city."

Rosie slipped on her parka and picked up her purse. "I have this lovely perfume…"

Mary shook her head. "No thank you," she said politely, but firmly. "This is a case. Nothing else."

They walked over to the door and Mary opened it, letting Bradley step in.

"Good morning, Rosie, Stanley. Good to see you."

"Disappointing," Stanley muttered, as he walked past Bradley. "Quite disappointing."

Rosie stopped and took a good look at Bradley. Her face lit up with sudden understanding. She patted Bradley on the shoulder. "It's okay, dear," she said. "You just be happy with who you are."

She turned to Mary, shook her head sadly and whispered loudly, "It's always the good-looking ones."

Bradley watched them both walk down the steps before closing the door and turning to Mary.

"Why do I feel like I've just walked into the middle of something I know nothing about?"

Mary laughed out loud. "Believe me, you don't want to know."

He shrugged. "Okay, I'll trust you on that. You ready to go?"

Mary nodded. "Yes, all packed and ready. Any problems with arranging time off?"

"No, I let them know I was following up on the Marcum case and they were more than willing to cover for me."

"They really are the good guys," Mary said.

Bradley smiled. "Yeah, and I'm beginning to think that my administrative assistant, Dorothy, doesn't think I'm nuts anymore."

"Well, we'll have to do something to change that," she said with a grin.

He shrugged. "Unfortunately, I don't think it will take much."

Laughing, they picked up Mary's gear and carried it to Bradley's four-wheel drive SUV. "Do you need to stop at your office before we leave town?" he asked.

Mary shook her head. "No, Rosie and Stanley are going to check calls for me. Andy is going to shovel for me. And Joey is going to find me in Chicago. I think things are set."

"Good, let's get going."

Chapter Ten

As they drove down South Street to Highway 20, Mary's cell phone rang. "It's Sean," she said to Bradley before answering the call.

"Hi, what's up?" she asked. "We are just getting on the road."

"We've made contact with the couple who was interested in the baby," he said. "They had a feeling that things weren't on the up and up. But they were more concerned about young mothers changing their minds, rather than any kind of criminal activity. When we told them the safety of the baby was concerned, they were willing to meet with us."

"That's great," Mary replied. "When are we meeting them? Should we go directly there?"

"No. Let's meet at the folks first," Sean said. "Then we'll talk with them later this afternoon. We're putting a tap on their phone and we've got someone from our unit with them. We're going to have them call the perps back and tell them they've changed their minds and they want the baby."

"You don't think the perps will be concerned they're being set up?" she asked.

"No, the couple said the perps told them to think about it and not make a hasty decision," he said. "So I think we're safe. But, just in case, is Joey still able to reach you?"

"Yes. Joey said once he made contact with me, he's able to find me no matter where I am."

"I've gotta tell you, sis. This is just too weird for me."

Mary laughed. "Yeah, for me too. But, hey, you play with the cards you're dealt."

"You're doing a great job," he said. "I don't know if I've told you I'm amazed at what you've done with your life."

"Thanks, Sean, that means a lot coming from you," she replied, her voice catching. "I'll see you in a couple of hours, okay?"

"Yeah," he replied. "See you then."

"Are you okay?" Bradley asked.

She turned and smiled at him. "Yeah, Sean was getting mushy, so I had to get off the phone before he embarrassed himself."

Bradley chuckled. "It's pretty sad to see those big manly types go soft."

"I know," Mary responded, as she wiped the tears from her eyes. "They make such a mess."

"So, what's up with the perps?" Bradley asked, hoping the change of topic would clear the emotion from her face.

"Great news," she said brightly. "They contacted the couple, who thought the whole adoption organization might have been suspicious. The couple is willing to cooperate with the police. We're going to meet with them this afternoon."

Bradley pulled onto Highway 20 and shifted into a lower gear. Mary sat up in her seat and looked around the snow-covered landscape. The road had been cleared of most of the accumulated snow, but was still covered with a layer of white. The divided highway wove through six-foot high drifts and an assortment of abandoned jack-knifed trucks and cars stuck in the ditch.

"Looks like there are a lot of people out there who drive like you," Bradley teased.

"I'd punch your arm," Mary said. "But you might lose control and we'd end up in there too."

Bradley laughed. "Saved by fear."

"This is one of the things I noticed when I moved out here," Mary said, looking out over the acres of farmland frosted in soft white peaks, "the openness. You don't have block after block of buildings. You can actually see for miles. In Chicago, you can only see for miles if you're at the top of one of the high skyscrapers."

He nodded. "I noticed the dark," he said. "In the city, there is so much additional light you only see the brightest stars. At night in Freeport it actually gets dark, dark enough to see hundreds of stars. You get to see what's really out there."

"Some people don't like to know what's really out there," Mary commented. "They would rather stay where the light shelters them from the truth."

"Mary O'Reilly, are you a philosopher?" Bradley teased.

She laughed. "No, just someone who has been spending a whole lot of time in the dark lately."

"Can I ask a personal question?" he asked.

"Sure."

"It seems to me that your brother, Sean, really cares about you."

"Yes, he does," she replied. "We're a very close-knit family."

Bradley nodded. "That's what I thought. So, why does he risk your safety by having you come into the city and work on a case?"

Mary looked out the window and sighed.

"He doesn't know how the spirits can overwhelm you, does he?"

Mary shook her head. "No, he doesn't. No one in the family knows except for my mother," she admitted.

"And she guessed it for herself," Bradley added.

Mary nodded and shrugged. "Yeah, she always knows more than we tell her."

"Why wouldn't you tell them?" he asked. "They would never..."

"Do you know what it's like being the little sister of three big brothers?" she interrupted. "No, of course not, because you would be one of the big brothers. Always protecting little Mary. Always watching out for little Mary. Always warning off the boys. Always telling me what I should and shouldn't do."

"Because they love you."

"Yes, I know," she said, "and that's what makes it even harder. They would smother me with

67

love. I finally, finally, received the respect and trust I wanted when I joined the force and received commendations for my work. I was finally one of them, not just a little sister. An equal. I don't want that to change."

She turned in her seat and met his eyes. "I don't want them to find out," she said. "I want you to keep my secret."

Bradley sighed. "Okay, I can understand your feelings," he said. "But I think you're making a mistake not telling them. However, I'm willing to do whatever it takes to help you keep your secret."

"Thanks, I really appreciate it."

He shrugged. "Hey, that's what friends do," he said.

"So, it's my turn," she said. "Can I ask you a personal question?"

He smiled. "Yes, my life is an open book."

"Would you tell me about your wife, Jeannine?"

Bradley nearly drove the SUV off the road. "What?"

Mary cringed. "If you don't want to talk about her…that's your prerogative."

He was silent for a few moments. Then he nodded absently. "No, it's fair," he said. "I put my nose into your business…"

Mary shook her head. "No, this isn't a game," she said. "Really, if talking about her causes you pain…"

"We were married for four years," he said. "We were high school sweethearts. She was a cheerleader..."

"And you were the football stud," Mary added.

Bradley looked at her and shook his head. "No, I was the clumsy, nerdy, math geek," he grinned at her, "but thanks!"

She shook her head. "I don't believe that. Come on, which position?"

He laughed. "Water boy."

"No! Really?"

"Yeah, I was the captain of the swim team," he said, "the original water boy."

The image of Bradley in a Speedo flashed across Mary's mind.

"I can picture you in Speedo," she said absently, her mind still focused on the mental image.

"What did you say?" Bradley asked.

Mary blushed. "I mean, I can see you as a swimmer."

Bradley chuckled. "I could lend you my high school yearbook if you'd like."

"Shut up," she said.

He laughed aloud. "Just trying to be helpful."

Mary snorted. "Continue with your story."

"I did my time in the military and when I was finished, I got accepted in the police force. We got married a week after I completed my training at the Police Academy. I had accepted a position with the DeKalb Police Department and Jeannine worked as a

69

veterinary assistant in Sycamore. We had a nice little house, some extra spending money, and good friends. I thought things were pretty great."

"But they weren't?"

Bradley smiled. "You know, you're using your interrogation tactics right now."

Mary blushed. "Sorry, hard habit to break."

He nodded. "Actually, that ended up being our problem too," he said.

"You would interrogate her?"

"No, I was just always on the job," he said. "Always a cop. Always casing the joint. Always on alert. And she was feeling left out."

"Yeah, sometimes I wonder how my mom does it," she said. "She's surrounded by cops. But she does insist we stop shop talk for a while and converse about other things."

"Does that work?"

Mary laughed. "For about fifteen minutes, then we're back at it."

"Yeah, Jeannine was trying to get me to do the same thing," he said. "But I wasn't as willing to let things go."

Bradley paused for a moment as he negotiated the entrance ramp from Highway 20 onto Interstate 90 going southeast into Chicago. The roads on the Interstate where much clearer and traffic was a little heavier. Bradley moved into the left lane, passed a few slower moving trucks and merged back into the right lane.

"She got my attention when she asked for a divorce," he said.

"That must have been a shock."

"It was a punch to the gut," he replied. "I honestly never thought it was that bad for her. I thought she'd just get used to my way of handling the job. But I was wrong."

"So, what did you do?"

Bradley shrugged. "I decided she...we...were more important than the job. It took me three years of married life to actually start acting like a husband. Six months later, she was pregnant and I was floating on air."

He drove for a few miles in silence. Mary watched as he worked to control his emotions.

"Six months after that, I lost her."

"She died?"

"I don't know. That's the hell of it. I got a call when I was on patrol that there was a breaking and entering, and then I heard my address. I don't even remember driving home. When I got there, the chief was at the front door to hold me back. He said he didn't want me storming around in there, messing up evidence."

"What happened?"

"I still don't know. The house was torn apart and Jeannine was gone. No notes, no kidnapping demands...no blood, thank God. But she was just gone. The chief asked me if she could have staged it, if she was unhappy with our life..."

71

His voice cracked and he tightened his grip on the steering wheel. He shook his head. "We had just found out we were expecting a little girl. We had just bought the pink wallpaper for her room. I was going to put the crib together that night. She was happy. I'm sure she was happy."

Mary reached over, placed her hand over his and squeezed. "I agree with you, she was happy and she wouldn't have left of her own free will," she said. "I'm not saying this as a friend who wants you to feel better, but as a trained professional. She didn't leave."

Bradley stared ahead at the roadway, but nodded his head. "Thanks. That means a lot to me."

They drove in silence until they reached a toll booth that flashed the Amber Alert about Jeremy across an electronic billboard.

"I searched for her," he said suddenly, "for eight years. I followed up on any leads, checked out all of the Jane Does, made calls and worked the case twenty-four-seven. I never came up with anything."

"So you don't know...?" Mary paused.

"Whether she's dead or alive? Whether I have an eight-year-old daughter out there somewhere? Whether she even remembers who she is?" He shook his head. "No, I don't know anything."

Mary looked out the window to the snow covered fields surrounding the highway. *How would it be to live each day, searching and not finding anything?*

"I think I'd go a little crazy," she murmured.

He nodded. "I think I did. I was totally obsessed. I lost my job, my house, my savings – trying to find them."

She shrugged. "What else could you do? You would have to do all you could."

He smiled. "Thanks, not many people understand."

He took a deep breath. "So, about eighteen months ago, I looked around and realized that I was no closer to finding her than I had been eight years before. I didn't have money or a job. And considering my recent history, it wasn't going to be easy for me to get another job."

"Why?"

"I went off the deep end with the investigation," he said. "I pestered the investigators, told them they didn't know what they were doing, interfered and generally made an ass of myself."

"It's hard when it's personal."

He nodded. "So when I contacted my captain, he made a call and I got the job in Freeport. I think I got the job because the mayor wanted to hire someone who was crazy. He didn't really like having a Police Chief who might catch on to him."

"Funny how things work out," Mary said.

He nodded. "Yeah, funny."

"You know, I was talking to Joey just before we left. Telling him that the phone number he got could have saved his brother's life. And then he said…" She paused as emotion choked her voice.

73

"What did he say, Mary?" Bradley asked gently.

"He said 'Good thing I died, huh?'" she replied softly.

"Damn. Do you really think that God allows bad things to happen to people in order to serve some grand plan in the future?"

Mary shook her head. "No, but I think God gives us opportunities to turn bad things into good things and make a difference in other people's lives."

They drove in silence for a few minutes.

"Mary, we are going to find Jeremy," he said.

Mary smiled. "Yes we are!"

Chapter Eleven

A narrow path had been plowed through the snow on the Chicago side street, enough for a car and a half to drive down. "This makes no sense whatsoever," Bradley said, navigating the four-wheel SUV around the cars coming from the opposite direction. "Why don't they just plow it wider?"

Mary smiled. "Welcome to Chicago."

She turned and looked out the window at the shoveled out parking spaces that either held vehicles or an assortment of chairs, tables or other large objects claiming ownership of the spot. One particularly religious person had placed a five-foot high statue of the Virgin Mary in their spot.

"Turn right at the corner," Mary instructed.

A few moments later they were in front of her parents' brick bungalow on the northwest side of the city. "We can park here," Mary said.

"What is that holding our place?" Bradley asked.

Mary laughed at the trio of plastic ghosts normally used for decorating the lawn at Halloween. "My brothers' sick idea of a joke," she said.

She hopped out of the car, moved the five foot high structure and stepped back so Bradley could park. He got out of the car with their gear and took a good look at the ghosts. "I think I'm going to like your brothers."

Mary nodded. "Yeah, that's what I'm afraid of."

No sooner had they walked up the steps than the door burst open and Mary was engulfed by a pair of strong arms that lifted off her feet. "Mary-Mary, it's great to have you home," her father said.

"Dad, I was home two days ago," Mary teased.

"Ah, but when you're here, the house seems a wee bit brighter."

She laughed and turned to Bradley. "Dad, this is my friend Bradley Alden. He's the Police Chief from Freeport. Bradley, my dad, Timothy O'Reilly."

Bradley stepped forward and extended his hand to the tall, burly Irishman. "A pleasure to meet you, sir."

His hand was accepted in a firm grip. "Good to meet you, young man."

Timothy smiled and placed his hand on Bradley's shoulder, ushering him into the house.

"Welcome to our home."

Margaret Katherine O'Reilly, Mary's mother, came bustling forward, her petite frame covered in an apron. With arms outstretched, she gave Mary a fierce hug. "Mary, so good to have you home again."

She turned to Bradley and, to his surprise, hugged him too. "Welcome," she said simply and Bradley, knowing she meant it, found he had to swallow a lump in his throat.

"Thank you, Mrs. O'Reilly."

She smiled. "Call me Maggie, everyone does."

The house was decorated in warm tones, with large, comfortable pieces of furniture. Mary's brothers, Arthur and Thomas, were seated in the living room watching a football game. "The Irish are down by three," Arthur called, "fourth quarter, twelve minutes to go."

"Oh, well, then, the rest of the world and good manners should just go by the wayside," Maggie said. "I'm ashamed that Mary's friend should see the kind of hooligans I've raised."

Arthur looked up at Bradley and grinned. "Hi, I'm the hooligan called Art," he said. "This is my hooligan twin, Thomas."

Bradley grinned. "Hi, I'm Bradley," he said and made a comment about Notre Dame's current quarterback.

"You know Notre Dame?" Thomas asked.

Bradley nodded. "Fighting Irish, oh, yeah."

Mary watched Bradley slide closer to the couch, trying to crane his neck to see the screen. "Sean isn't here yet," she said. "If you'd like to watch the game until he comes, that would be fine."

"Really?" he asked, a happy grin spread across his face.

Mary nodded. "Really."

"Hey, Bradley, have a seat," Art called.

Soon all four men were seated on the couch yelling at the television screen. Maggie rolled her eyes. "Well, there's no use for sensible people in this room," she said. "Let's go into the kitchen and have a chat.

"He's a nice young man, your Bradley," Maggie said, as she poured Mary a cup of tea. "I like his eyes."

Mary smiled and shook her head. "Mom, he's not *my* anything," she said, "except a good friend."

Maggie shrugged. "So, how was your drive in?" she asked. "Did you have any troubles?"

Mary shook her head. "No," she said quickly, and then paused. "Mom...no...we had no problems at all. I've never driven in without at least one sighting."

Maggie smiled. "Is that right? Hmmmm, I wonder what caused the change?"

"Oh, no, it wasn't Bradley, Mom," she said. "In the real world, fairy tales don't work."

Maggie laughed. "Mary, in the real world people don't talk to ghosts."

Bradley sat back on the couch and relaxed. The Fighting Irish had scored another touchdown and were now up by four. The announcer had paused for a station break and a commercial about a popular beer was playing on the screen. He turned to the other men with a pleasant expression on his face, to be met with three pairs of solemn eyes assessing him.

"And how did you meet our Mary?" Art asked, going immediately to the point.

Bradley sat up on the couch. "We met working on her last case," he replied.

"And you'd never seen her before that?" Thomas asked.

He thought about the jogging encounters he and Mary had for several months before he actually knew who she was.

"Well, actually, I had seen her before I officially met her," he admitted. "We would jog at the same time in the park."

"Ahhh, jogging," Art said. "Girls dressed in those cute little spandex shorts and sports bras. Could make a man yearn for exercising every day."

Bradley started to smile; then, remembering who he was talking to, remained straight-faced. "Well, I could tell she took exercising seriously."

Thomas snorted. "And how could you tell that?"

Damn, he thought. *What do I say to avoid getting my butt kicked by three big Irish cops?*

"Because she beat me in a race nine times out of ten," he admitted. "And it was slightly humiliating."

"That's our Mary," Thomas said, with more than a little pride. "Always wanted to be first, fastest and best. I hated when she beat me."

Art laughed and slapped Bradley on the shoulder. "I'm in complete sympathy with you," he said. "She enjoys showing men up. It's disgusting."

The game started up again and the men turned back to the screen. Bradley sat back, feeling like part of the group once again. *That went really well.*

"So," Thomas said nonchalantly. "How many times have you spent the night at our Mary's place?"

Bradley shrugged, his eyes on the quarterback weaving his way through the other team's defensive line. "Just a couple of times," he said absently.

Three pairs of eyes turned from the screen back to him.

Crap.

Before the men could respond, the front door opened and another Irish giant entered the house. *Great, another one. I don't stand a chance.*

Sean O'Reilly walked across the room and stood before Bradley. "You must be Chief Alden," he said. "I understand you saved our Mary's life last month. I'd like to shake your hand."

Bradley stood and extended his hand. "I don't know where you got your information," he said, "but I think your sister was the one who saved my life."

Sean shook his head. "Let's see if I can recall all the facts," he said. "Someone shot at her in town; you pushed her down and covered her with your body. Someone was shooting at her in a forest preserve; you showed up in a knick of time to scare the fellow off. A serial killer breaks into her house while she's in the shower; you pound on the door, scare him off and then spend the night on the couch protecting her. And then finally, you take a shot in the foot after you are both abducted and you make her leave you behind. Do I have the facts right?"

Bradley shrugged. "Really, it sounds like a big deal, but Mary has pulled me out of some pretty tight spots too."

Timothy stood and put his arm around Bradley. "You did that for our little girl?"

"Yes, he did," Sean said. "And he insisted on driving her in today."

"Mary let you drive?" Art said in awe. "You're a better man than I."

Bradley smiled. "It wasn't easy, but her car was slightly out of commission."

"Parked sideways in her drive," Sean said, to his brothers' delight.

Bradley shook his head. "Do you have spies in Freeport?"

Sean simply smiled and shrugged.

"Hello, remember me?"

Bradley looked around Sean to see another man closing the front door behind him. He was nearly as tall as the O'Reilly men, but instead of being big-boned and burly, he was muscled and slim. He had dark wavy hair, bright blues eyes and a smile that belonged on a toothpaste commercial. This was going to be Mary's husband? Bradley hated him already.

Mary and Maggie walked into the room.

"Kevin!" Mary yelled and threw herself into the arms of the man.

What the hell? Bradley thought.

Kevin lifted Mary in his arms and hugged her tightly. Then he loosened his hold and placed her back on the ground to get a good look at her. "Well, little O'Reilly has grown up to be hot," he said with a grin.

Bradley didn't like his grin.

Mary smiled. "You used to call me a brat," she reminded him.

"Oh, darling, you can't hold that against me," he said. "I was only sixteen and you, as I recall, were ten…and a brat."

"Okay, I admit I could have been a brat occasionally," Mary said, laughing, "but it wasn't nice of you to point it out."

He lifted her hand to his lips, turned it over and placed a kiss in her palm. "You're right," he said. "Please accept my humble apology. I was a boorish youth."

And you're not much better all grown up, Bradley thought.

"Well, since you asked so nicely," she said. "And…"

"We are to be man and wife, so we should really start the relationship off as…" He interrupted her, lifted her other hand and placed a kiss on it. "…at the very least…friends."

Okay, enough is enough. "Um, perhaps we ought to discuss the case," Bradley said to no one in particular.

Sean grinned. "Okay, Kevin, get your hands off my kid sister and let's get to work."

Kevin grinned. "Can you blame a guy?" he asked, wrapping his arm around Mary's waist.

Yeah, I can! Bradley thought, walking across the room and standing in front of the cozy couple. "Hi, I don't think we've been introduced yet," he said, extending his hand. "I'm Bradley Alden, Chief of Police in Freeport, and a *good* friend of Mary's."

Kevin unwrapped his arm from Mary's waist and shook Bradley's hand. "Hi, Sergeant Kevin Brady, Vice Squad, Chicago Police Department, family friend and Mary's *new husband*," he replied.

Before he could place his arm back around Mary, Bradley moved between them and placed his arm around her shoulders. "Mary, why don't you sit down over here and then we can discuss the case?"

With a slightly smug grin, Bradley guided Mary through the front room and into a recliner, situated a little way from the other furniture in the room. Then he sat on the floor at her feet. "So, Sean," he said with a smile. "What's the next step?"

Sean grinned and sat on the couch. "Have a seat, Kev," he offered. "We can't waste any more time."

Kevin leaned against the doorway and nodded. "I'm fine here, Sean," he said. "Let's get down to business."

Bradley leaned back against the recliner and brought his arm up, so it rested on Mary's knees. "I agree, let's get down to business."

As Sean brought Kevin up to speed on the case, Bradley's attention was caught by a movement outside the house. He thought he saw someone standing outside the house, trying to peer into the window.

"What?" Mary whispered, feeling the tension in his body.

He quickly shook his head, stood up and walked to the window. Peering out, he couldn't see anyone and there were no tracks on the snow either.

Must have been my imagination.

When he turned from the window, he saw that Kevin had taken his place next to Mary.

Well, this is going to be an interesting couple of days.

Chapter Twelve

"So, Bradley and Mary will get settled into to their rooms at the hotel," Sean said. "We will all meet at the Martin's place at four-thirty and then we can catch some dinner after that. Any questions?"

"Don't you think that Mary and I need some alone time so we give the appearance of a couple in love?" Kevin asked, smiling up at Mary.

"No." Sean and Bradley said simultaneously.

Sean looked across the room to Bradley with a lifted eyebrow. Bradley merely shrugged.

"We need to get them settled and get going," Sean said. "If you can't fake it, I'll have Bradley act as her husband and you can work back up with me."

"I can do it," Kevin said, shrugging. "But you can't blame a guy for trying." He squeezed Mary's knee. "We'll be sure to take some time later to get reacquainted," he offered.

Like hell. "So, Sean, where are Mary and I setting up?" Bradley asked, walking over to help Mary out of the chair.

"I've got you a couple of rooms at a place downtown," Sean said. "Here's the address. We'll see you at four-thirty."

Bradley nodded. "Great."

After their goodbyes, Sean, Kevin, Bradley and Mary walked to their respective cars. The snow was falling again, but this time the flakes were tiny glittering flecks. Mary turned and smiled at Bradley, her hair dusted with a frosty shimmer. "It's like fairy dust," she said.

"Great, just what we need, more magic," he growled with a smile.

Laughing, she quickly turned and started to slip. Bradley quickly grabbed her arm and held her upright. "My hero," she teased.

"Yeah, just don't forget it," he murmured.

"Excuse me?" Mary asked.

"I said 'get in,'" so you're out of the cold."

Mary's eyes sparkled up at him and she bit back a grin. "Sure you did."

As he helped her into the car, he glanced over to Sean and Kevin, deep in conversation. Standing next to Kevin was the woman he had seen in the window and, as the snow fell through her, he could easily tell that she was a ghost. She was young, perhaps sixteen or seventeen. She looked like she was Hispanic – she had been a beautiful girl. Now her face was blue and her clothing was dripping wet. But even more interesting to Bradley was the fact that she was looking at Kevin like a woman in love.

Mary slipped her arm out of his grip and the woman faded away. "What?" she asked.

"I thought I saw something," he said.

"Where?" she asked.

Bradley shook his head, the last thing Mary needed right now was another case to solve. He'd check into it later with Sean. "Never mind, it was nothing," he said. "Let's get downtown."

He climbed in to the car and started it.

"What did you see?" she insisted.

Bradley pulled away from the curb, carefully navigating down the narrow street and then onto the highway entrance ramp. "I'll tell you about it later," he said. "How was your visit with your mom?"

"I know you're trying to change the subject," Mary said. "But that's okay, because I wanted to talk to you about something my mom suggested."

"I like your mom, by the way," he said. "She's a nice lady."

Mary smiled. "Thanks, I think so too. My brothers and I are lucky."

"So, what did she suggest?"

"She asked me about our trip in from Freeport and when I answered, I realized I didn't have one sighting, nothing paranormal at all."

"Is that normal?"

Mary shook her head. "No, I've never had a trip without seeing at least one ghost and usually much more," she admitted. "This was certainly unusual."

"Could it have been the snowstorm, you know, barometric pressure?" he suggested.

"No, I've driven in snowstorms before."

"Well, you weren't driving, I was. Could that make a difference?"

"No, I've been a passenger and had sightings."

"So, what are the other conditions that were unique for the drive this morning?"

"The only thing I can think of is you," she said.

"Well, thanks, Mary, that is flattering and everything. But really, you should be thinking about what keeps the ghosts away."

Mary laughed. "You...your presence was the only change from my other trips," she said.

"So, you don't only think about me?" he asked with mock despair.

She chuckled. "So, how do you chase my ghosts away, Bradley Alden?"

He shook his head. "Well, it's obvious I don't chase all the ghosts away, because they have come when I've been with you."

Mary thought about it. "But they've been with me first. I don't think I've had a ghost that isn't already connected with me show up when you are around."

"So, I'm the paranormal equivalent of bug repellent?"

She shook her head. "No, because they don't run away when you come into the room. This is very interesting."

"But at this point, it's only a hypothesis," he said. "We really don't have any solid facts proving it. You're just assuming I can ward them away because of one isolated situation. I think I'm going to need more proof before I'm convinced."

He drove onto the exit ramp to Ohio Street, entering the outskirts of downtown Chicago.

"Well, we do have another case of ghosts not appearing," she said. "The drive between my parents' home and downtown. No specters on the horizon."

"Could be the car," Bradley suggested. "Perhaps something in the car is vibrating causing a spectrum of harmonic sound waves that repel ghosts."

"Wow! You're really exploring all the angles on this one," she said.

Bradley turned and met her eyes for a moment. "Mary, this is about your safety," he said. "Do you think I wouldn't take that seriously?"

She was touched. "Okay, we have a little time, why don't you pull over and let's test it out?" Mary suggested.

"What do you mean?"

Mary shrugged. "I'll get out of the car and walk for a while. See what happens," she said. "Then after a block or so, you catch up to me and we see what happens."

Bradley pondered her suggestion for a moment. "You said that once a ghost connects with you, it doesn't matter if I'm there or not," he pointed out. "So, how can we tell if it's me? The ghosts will still be there."

Shaking her head, Mary responded, "No, just seeing the ghosts doesn't cause a connection. I have to acknowledge them. Say something to them. Interact in some way."

"So, even if they know you can see them, they're not connected with you, right?"

"Right."

Bradley turned right onto LaSalle and drove down a block and a half before he could find an open parking spot. "Okay," he said. "You get out and start walking down the street and I'll watch you for thirty seconds. Then I'll follow you. Remember, no connections."

Mary exited the SUV and closed the door firmly behind her. As soon as she stepped onto the street she began to see the strange "layering" of time periods as ghosts walked into her line of vision. The modern buildings faded out and were replaced with wide open prairies with an American Indian Scouting Party running by. That faded and Mary watched fur traders portaging their canoes as they headed to the shores of Lake Michigan. Soon they faded away to be replaced by cobbled streets and wooden tenement buildings. The acrid smell of smoke was heavy in the air and people were rushing around her with wooden buckets filled with water. Then a stylish flapper and her date strolled down the street until they surreptitiously slipped down a short flight of steps to a heavy wooden door. The gentleman knocked three times and a small window in the center of the door slid open. Moments later, the couple entered the speakeasy.

The time period moved to more contemporary times. Mary saw her share of street people, prostitutes and pimps, gang bangers and distraught businessmen fade in and out of the scene before her. Finally, she noticed an altogether different group of ghosts.

Dogs, all shapes and sizes, and cats of every variety were moving within the crowds of people walking down the street. These invisible pets rubbed themselves against the busy pedestrians, cats purring loudly and dogs, with their tails wagging, looked beseechingly into the faces of the living humans on their way to work or shopping.

Mary turned and realized that she was standing in front of the Anti-Cruelty Society. These were the animals that had never found a family and died in the care of the society. Even in death, they longed to belong to someone. Mary felt a tug and looked down to see a large Golden Retriever playfully pulling on the corner of her coat. He dropped the coat and smiled up at her, his tongue lolling happily to the side. She bent down and patted his silken head.

"You're a charmer, aren't you," she whispered.

He barked and wagged his tail in response.

Suddenly, the rest of the cats and dogs faded away. The drunk, who had slipped through several cars on his way back to the bar, disappeared. The prostitute who had leaned forward on a car stopped for the light vanished.

Mary turned and saw Bradley standing next to her.

"So, I'm a charmer?" he asked, one eyebrow raised.

She smiled. "Actually, I was talking to someone else."

He looked concerned. "The deal was no connections," he said.

"Don't worry, I didn't make a connection. I only patted a sweet dog."

"Dogs can be ghosts?"

Mary shrugged. "Why not? They have spirits too."

Bradley shook his head. "Yeah, why not?"

He put his hand on her arm and guided her back to the SUV. "So, how did our experiment go?"

"Well, I received a mini lesson on the history of Chicago. But everyone faded away when you came close," she replied. "I don't understand the reasons, but you seem to discourage unwanted paranormal advances."

He smiled. "I'm sure it's my brawny, tough exterior."

"Or your breath."

Bradley breathed into his cupped hand. "Really, my breath…"

Mary laughed. "Joking, just joking."

"Funny," he replied, putting the SUV in drive and slipping back into the flow of traffic. "So, tell me about you and hotel rooms."

"I beg your pardon," she sputtered.

He chuckled. "Sorry, I meant are you bothered by ghosts in hotel rooms or are you fine?"

"Oh," Mary blushed, suddenly wishing that she too could fade away like the ghosts she had just seen. "I don't really know. I haven't stayed in a hotel since I was shot."

"Then let's see if we can upgrade to a suite," he suggested. "That way, I'm close, but not invading your space."

"Thanks. That would be nice."

"So, is Kevin going to be staying with us too?" he asked casually.

Mary shook her head. "No, he has his own place. Sean didn't really feel the need to have us living together."

Bradley nodded and hid a smile. "I wanted to tell you that I really liked your family," he said, adding under his breath, "especially Sean."

Chapter Thirteen

"What was he thinking?" Mary asked in dismay as they pulled up to the hotel.

"What?" Bradley asked, confusion clearly showing on his face.

"This is the Congress Plaza Hotel," she replied. "The most haunted hotel in Chicago."

"Ahhh, well perhaps he thought that you would enjoy it because you're not afraid of ghosts," he offered.

"Or perhaps he thought it would be a good joke," she countered.

Bradley nodded. "Yeah, that could have been it too. Do you want to find another place to stay?"

She shook her head. "No, I can deal with it," she said, smiling over her shoulder at him. "Good thing I brought you along."

He smiled back. "Yeah, remember that, okay?"

Bradley held back a whistle as he walked into the ornate lobby. Marble floors and pillars, tall ceilings replete with mosaic tiles, highly polished counters and a sense of resplendence expected for a showcase hotel built in 1893. "Like stepping back in time," he said.

Mary nodded. "Al Capone used this place for his business meetings. There are secret passages between this and several other buildings in downtown Chicago."

"Did Al tell you that himself?"

"Cute, Bradley. Cute!"

After a quick conversation with the reservations clerk, they were upgraded to a suite. On the way to the elevators Bradley heard his name called.

"Officer Alden, is that you?"

Bradley turned to watch a tall, slinky blonde in high heels and a long fur coat glide across the lobby toward them. She wrapped her arms around Bradley's neck and kissed him passionately on the lips.

Stunned, Bradley stepped back. "I'm sorry," he stammered. "Do I know you?"

Mary snorted. "Seems kind of obvious to me," she murmured.

The blonde's face fell. "You don't remember me? I'm Lily. You know, Lily from Heartbreakers Gentlemen's Club? You busted me about ten years ago."

"Hi, Lily, how've you been?" Bradley asked.

Lily perked up. "Oh, much better," she said. "I took your advice."

"I gave you advice?"

She giggled, high-pitched and nervous. "Yeah, of course you did," she said. "You told me that I was much better than that kind of place. You told me I needed to clean myself up and get a respectable job."

"Good advice," Mary said.

Lily beamed at Mary and opened her coat to reveal a very voluptuous body stuffed into some barely there lingerie. "I'm a personal escort now," she purred. "I'm making much better money and my clients treat me like the lady I am. You were right."

"Lily, I told you to wait for me over here," a rough male voice echoed in the lobby.

A bruiser, who could have easily been the entire defensive line for the Chicago Bears by himself, marched over. He wrapped a beefy hand around Lily's tiny arm and started to pull. Lily slapped his hand and surprisingly, he released her arm.

"Stop it, Marty, this is my friend, Officer Alden, from DeKalb," she said. "He was the one who got me into the business."

Bradley choked. "No, well, actually," he said. "This isn't exactly what I had in mind."

Mary had to bite the inside of her lip to keep from laughing.

"Batolli ain't gonna be real happy with you talking to the cops," Marty said.

"He ain't a cop, he's a friend," Lily tried to explain.

"He's a cop," Marty said. "I can smell them a mile away."

Lily folded her skinny arms over her ample chest. "Eddie won't care," she said. "He knows I'm loyal to him. Besides, he knows about Officer Alden."

"He does?" Mary asked.

Lily smiled. "Oh, yeah, Officer Alden was the one who got him busted when he was a kid. He told me that when he meets up with you again, he was gonna thank you for all of those years in the slammer."

"Lily, you bimbo, Eddie didn't mean it like that," Marty said, rolling his eyes in exasperation. "Eddie wanted to get even with him. Like take him out."

Lily's eyes widened. "No? Gosh, I'm sorry, Officer Alden, I don't want you to get shot or nothing."

"That's okay, Lily," Bradley said. "I'm not worried about Eddie Batolli."

"You should be worried about him," Marty threatened.

"Maybe it would be better if you don't mention to Eddie that Officer Alden is in town," Mary suggested.

"Now, why would I want to do that?" Marty asked, turning to Mary.

"You heard of Sean O'Reilly?" Mary asked calmly.

Marty nodded. "Yeah, I heard of O'Reilly. Mean SOB."

Mary nodded. "And my brother," she said. "I don't think Eddie wants an entire task force investigating his dealings, does he?"

She pulled out her cell phone. "I could call Sean right now and get things going."

Marty blanched. "Yeah, Eddie don't need to know about Alden. Best for all involved."

He grabbed Lily's arm. "Come on, you got an appointment."

"Bye, Officer Alden," Lily waved as she was pulled across the marble floor. "Good to see you again."

"You have the most interesting friends," Mary commented.

"Yeah, you don't know the half of it," Bradley muttered. "Let's get upstairs before something else happens."

Upstairs they unlocked the door to the Lakefront Suite, which offered two bedrooms, a parlor and a breathtaking view of Buckingham Fountain and Lake Michigan. Mary dropped her bags on the floor and walked to the window. The fountain, shut down for the winter, was covered with several inches of snow and the lake waters were choppy and gray. "Too bad it's not summer," she said.

Bradley joined her at the window. "I bet watching the fireworks from here would be incredible," he said.

"Wow, this place is so cool!"

Mary turned when she heard Joey's voice next to her. She placed her hand on Bradley's shoulder and motioned to where Joey stood at the window.

"This is amazing, isn't it?" he asked Bradley.

Bradley nodded. "Yeah, it's even better in the summer. That fountain over there has a light show where different colors are projected onto the flowing water. It's incredible."

Bradley heard another noise, looked across the room and then back at Mary. "Why do we have a dog?"

Crap, Mary thought. *I figured I could sneak that one by him. Should have known better.*

"A dog!" Joey squealed with delight and dashed across the room to where the Golden Retriever Mary met earlier that day sat in excited anticipation. They greeted each other as only a young boy and a big dog can, with hugs and kisses, wags and licks.

"He followed me home?" Mary said to Bradley.

"I distinctly remembered agreeing to no contact," he responded.

Mary grinned. "Yeah, but he was so cute."

Bradley laughed. "Like an eight-hundred-pound gorilla is cute. At least he won't eat much."

"And you don't have to walk him," Mary added.

She glanced over at Joey and the dog, rolling on the floor together. "Have you ever witnessed such complete and unadulterated joy?"

Bradley shook his head. "No, I haven't. But I think we're going to have to break up the party and discover why Joey came to see us in the first place."

"Oh, you're right," Mary said. "Joey, did you have something to report about Jeremy?"

Joey sat up, his arms still wrapped around the dog's neck. "Yeah," he said with a breathless smile, "the bad people are really happy again. They are treating Jeremy real good. They're even getting a babysitter to watch him while they go for a meeting tomorrow."

"They're not going to take Jeremy with them?" Bradley asked.

Joey shook his head. "No, they said they could get more for him if they held back. They said something about milk."

Mary nodded. "Yeah, milking the couple for more money. This is not going to be as straight-forward as we thought."

Joey stood up and walked over to them, the dog followed closely behind. "Is this bad for Jeremy?"

Bradley and Mary shook their head simultaneously. "No," Mary said. "It just means that they want more money, that's all."

"It's pretty common with people like this," Bradley added. "They get greedy. So, actually, because they think they can get more money for Jeremy, he's even safer."

Joey smiled. "That's good news."

He looked longingly at the dog. "I guess I should go back, huh?"

Mary nodded. "Sorry, Joey, but we really need you there to tell us if anything goes wrong. But you can come back and play with the dog later."

"What's his name?" Joey asked.

"He doesn't have one yet," she confessed, "so you get to name him."

"Really?" Joey asked. "That would be so cool. I never got to name a dog before."

"I'm sure he's happy he will be the first one you get to name."

Joey ran over and gave the dog a big hug, turned to Mary and Bradley with a big smile and faded away. The dog whined for a moment, they went to the corner of the room and lay down.

"Sorry, boy," Mary said. "He has to go for a while, but he'll be back."

Mary took her hand off Bradley's shoulder, walked over to her suitcase and carried it toward one of the bedrooms.

"I can smell dog," Bradley said. "Even though I can't see him, I can smell him."

"You're imagining things," she said. "You can't smell ghosts."

He followed her into the room. "Sure you can," he said. "It's called Olfactory Paranormal Phenomena."

She placed her suitcase on the bed and looked over to him. "Okay, that was impressive," she said. "You've been doing a little homework."

He folded his arms. "I can smell dog," he repeated.

"Well, if you can find a groomer who will wash a ghost dog, I'll be happy to bring him there," she said.

"He's sleeping in your room," he said.

"He's sleeping wherever he wants," she replied. "You can't really lock a ghost dog into a room."

Bradley ran his hand through his hair. "I can never win, can I?"

Mary smiled. "The best thing to do is just get used to it."

Chapter Fourteen

The young couple, otherwise known as "the pigeons," was actually Abby and Josh Martins. They were young professionals who worked and lived in downtown Chicago, in a trendy, upscale condo near Printer's Row, only a ten minute cab ride for Mary and Bradley. Sitting together in a love seat in their living room, it was obvious they also had an affection and love for each other that would make them perfect parents, eventually.

"We didn't realize the organization was criminal," Abby explained, holding tightly to Josh's hand. "We just answered an ad on Craigslist about an easier adoption process. I guess we should have known."

Mary, seated between Bradley and Kevin across from Abby on a leather couch, shook her head. "These people specialize in manipulating your emotions," she said. "They tell you what you want to hear and they make it sound so perfect."

"Too good to be true," Josh said. "That's what made us nervous."

"Well, your nervous reaction may be what will help us stop these criminals and reunite some babies with their real parents," Sean said, standing behind the couch. "Can you tell us what contact you've had with them so far?"

"The only contact has been through e-mails and phone calls," Josh said. "I've printed out all the e-mails and we've tried to remember what was said during the phone calls. Abby was better at remembering than me, but we wrote those down too."

"Great, this will be very helpful," Sean said.

"So, they've never met you?" Bradley asked. "They don't know what you look like?"

"No, we didn't even describe ourselves, just said that we wanted a Caucasian baby, a boy, and it really didn't matter his hair color," Abby said, her voice quivering. "We never thought they'd steal a baby for us."

"Of course you didn't," Mary said. "You were trying to invite a baby into your home, one you thought needed a home."

Abby nodded. "We thought they worked with young single mothers," she said.

"There are many agencies that do just that very thing," Bradley said. "If you'd like, we can get you in touch with some of those agencies. I have a feeling that a baby brought into this home would be very lucky."

Abby smiled. "Thank you."

"When did you first contact the agency?" Kevin asked.

"Around the first of October," Josh answered. "We just happened to be reading through Craigslist and found their ad."

"Was it an e-mail reply or a phone?" Kevin asked.

"The first time it was an e-mail," Josh said. "Then they called and sent us some paperwork."

"What information did you share with them?"

"Everything," Abby replied. "Our personal financial information, job information, credit information. I just realized how much confidential information they have about us."

"You might want to change any account numbers you gave to them," Kevin suggested. "And we can put you in touch with some people about safeguarding your identities."

Josh sighed. "I can't believe we were foolish enough to do this."

Mary smiled. "I guess you wanted a baby pretty badly."

Abby nodded. "Yes, we really did."

"Well, if you believe in Karma, you should be getting your baby," Mary replied, "since you are helping to get another one back home."

Abby smiled. "Thanks, Mary," she said, "that helps. So, you and Bradley are going to be playing me and Josh?"

Mary shook her head. "No, Kevin and I are going to be playing you two."

"Really?" Abby asked. "I thought it would be you and Bradley for sure; you have such a good connection."

Josh nodded. "I agree," he said. "You two seem more like a couple than you and Kevin."

Sean walked over and stood next to the loveseat, facing Bradley, Mary and Kevin. "Mary,

105

lean over and hold Kevin's hand, like Abby and Josh are doing," he said.

Mary dutifully placed her hand in Kevin's. He interlinked their fingers and brought her hand up to his lips. "I personally think we are the perfect couple," he said with a smile.

Mary smiled back and tried to relax and feel comfortable with Kevin.

Sean shook his head. "Okay, now let go of Kevin and lean over and link hands with Bradley."

Mary leaned toward Bradley and placed her hand in his. He turned to her, smiled and tucked her hand into both of his. She felt warmth course through her body and immediately relaxed. Bradley looked over and saw the young Hispanic girl standing in the room with them.

"Pretend you are Abby and Josh and talk about the baby you've always wanted," Sean prompted.

Mary turned, looked into Bradley's eyes and saw the quick flash of pain. "I don't think this is a good idea," Mary said. "Kevin and I…"

Bradley tightened the hold on her hand. "It's okay, Mary, really. Let's see if we can do this and convince Abby and Josh."

He slipped one hand out of the clasp and wrapped it around Mary's shoulders. "We always wanted a baby," he said. "I thought a girl would be great, with Abby's eyes and her smile. But she insisted we needed a boy, so I would have someone to play football with. She hates playing football with me."

Mary smiled. "Only because he's a sore loser when I beat him. I figured he'd at least have a couple of years before the baby kicks his butt."

Bradley laughed. "Until he's eight?" he asked.

She shrugged. "Well, maybe six," she replied.

Sean turned to Abby and Josh and nodded. "Yeah, you're right," he said. "These two are definitely going to be the husband and wife team. Their chemistry is perfect," he said. "Sorry, Kevin, you're going to be pulling back-up with me."

"Not only do I not get the girl, I get you?" Kevin asked with mock disgust. "Boy, did I volunteer for the wrong assignment."

"Sorry, Kevin," Bradley said with a grin.

"What time is the meeting?" Mary interrupted.

"Tomorrow morning, ten o'clock at the art museum," Abby said. "We are supposed to meet them in Gallery 240 in front of *A Sunday on La Grande Jatte* by Georges Seurat."

"I know the place," Mary said. "It's fairly public, but also provides a little privacy."

A few minutes later, the meeting ended. The officer Sean assigned to the Martins resumed her post and Mary, Bradley, Sean and Kevin moved the strategic planning meeting to Pizzeria Uno on Ohio Street. Their order placed, they turned the conversation to the meeting the next morning.

"The art museum is a funny place to bring a baby," Sean commented.

"They're not bringing the baby," Mary said. "Joey met us at the hotel and told us they've lined up a babysitter for Jeremy and are planning on milking the pigeons for more money."

"Who the hell is Joey?" Kevin asked.

Mary looked over at Sean with a raised eyebrow. *How much does Kevin know?* she wondered.

"He's an insider," Sean said. "He can only give us limited information."

So, he doesn't know all that much, Mary thought. *And for some reason, Sean doesn't want him to know any more.*

Bradley reached over and took Mary's hand in his. "The truth is, Kevin, I'm a psychic. Joey is the baby's brother who died this summer," Bradley said. "He's our inside man."

Kevin snorted. "You're kidding, right?" he said, looking around the room. "What is this, some kind of reality TV show?"

Bradley shook his head. "No, I just happen to be able to see dead people and they talk to me."

"So prove it," Kevin said. "Are there any ghosts in the room?"

Bradley shrugged and looked around. "Well, over in the corner is a cop, a sergeant," he said. "He just walked by the table. Last name was Monroe. Looks to be about forty...kind of heavy. He smiled at you and Sean – so I guess you knew him."

"Damn, wasn't Monroe your partner, Kev? Didn't he keel over last year in this place?" Sean asked, moving around in his seat to look at the corner Bradley had motioned toward. "He was eating deep-dish and his heart finally gave out."

Kevin's face turned pale. "So, what did he say to you?" he asked.

"He didn't talk to me at all," Bradley said. "Not all ghosts talk to me. Only when they need me to help them figure something out – like helping a baby brother."

"Or solving a murder," Sean added. "Like you did in Freeport last month."

So Sean's playing along; this is interesting, Bradley thought.

"They walk up to you and tell you who killed them?" Kevin asked. "Sounds like pretty easy gig, but it doesn't hold up too well in court."

"Well, not all ghosts remember who killed them," Mary added, "from what Bradley has told me. But they can help lead us to clues that help solve cases."

"So, Mary, you actually believe in this stuff?" Kevin asked.

Mary grinned. "Oh, yeah, I'm a believer."

Kevin shook his head. "This is totally crazy," he said. "But, hey, crazier things have happened."

Bradley turned to Sean. "Looks like our order is up," he said. "Sean, want to give me a hand?"

Sean and Bradley walked to the bar. "So, why don't you want Kevin to know about Mary?" Bradley asked.

"We all, the family, agreed that it would be better to keep her talents under cover," he said. "People get nervous when they're confronted with something unusual, especially people who have something to hide. So, the fewer who know, the less chance of it getting spread around."

Bradley nodded. "That makes sense," he said. "It's not Kevin. You trust him?"

Sean grinned. "Kev's a good guy. I've known him since grade school. He was a couple years younger than me, but always someone I could trust. He's highly respected in the force too. Little bit of a ladies' man, but yeah, if there were anyone we could trust with Mary's information it would be Kevin."

They picked up the pizza and appetizers and headed back to the table.

Mary was confused. As soon as Bradley was far enough away, she was able to see the ghosts in the room. She saw the cop Bradley had seen and wondered how Bradley knew he was there. She also saw a young woman standing next to their table, a Hispanic girl who looked as if she might have been a prostitute when she was alive.

"So, what have you been working on lately?" she asked Kevin.

"You know, the fun stuff," he replied with a grin. "Drugs and sex."

"The fun stuff?" she asked. "You have a strange idea of fun."

He paused for a moment and reached across the table for her hands. "Actually, things aren't going great in my life," he said. "I was trying to help a young prostitute and things went wrong. Very wrong. She ended up missing. I'm guessing she's dead."

Mary squeezed his hands. "I am so sorry," she said. "I know how that feels. But Kevin, I'm sure you did everything you could."

He shook his head. "Yeah, I did. But it still hurts. I got the feeling she had a crush on me. She was so cute. Like a puppy dog. I only wish I knew what happened to her."

"I can..." Mary started, and then paused. "I can ask Bradley to look for you. If she was connected to you, she might be nearby. He'll be able to help you find her and discover what happened to her."

Kevin smiled. "Really?" he asked. "Bradley can do all that."

"Yes, he's very good at discovering secrets."

"That's a good talent to have," Kevin agreed, "especially in police work."

"It has come in handy. More than once."

The conversation ended when Sean and Bradley came back with the dinner. "Hey, what are you two chatting about?" Sean asked.

"Just catching up," Kevin said, releasing Mary's hands and sitting back in his chair. "I didn't realize just how much I missed seeing Mary. That's something I hope to remedy."

Bradley sat down next to Mary, and placed his arm causally along the back of her chair. "Well, it's a bit of a drive to Freeport," he said, "but we'd love to show you the sights if you decide to make the trip."

Kevin glanced at Bradley, and then turned his attention to Mary. "So, are you involved with anyone at the moment?"

Mary involuntarily glanced at Bradley and then at Kevin. "No, nothing official," she said and felt her heart drop when Bradley moved his arm from the back of the chair.

"Oh?" Kevin asked with a smile. "I got the feeling that you and Bradley…"

"We're friends," Mary said, smiling a little too brightly. "Good friends."

Kevin leaned forward and placed his hand over Mary's. "That's music to my ears."

Chapter Fifteen

"Well, this certainly has been an interesting evening," Mary said as they entered their hotel suite later that evening.

"Have you and Kevin known each other for very long?" Bradley asked.

She shrugged. "He was one of the neighborhood kids," she said. "He liked to hang out at our house with my brothers."

Yeah, while trying to get close to the sister, Bradley thought.

She sat on the large couch that faced the window. Bradley sat on a chair adjacent to the couch, his feet propped on the coffee table.

"Thanks for stepping in when I slipped the information about Joey," she said. "Sean doesn't like telling people about my talents. But he was fine with you pretending to be the one with psychic ability. I don't understand him."

Bradley smiled. "I do," he said. "He was protecting his sister. Sean doesn't want anyone worried that you can see their dirty little secrets."

Mary sat back on the couch and sighed. "Should I say the obvious, that really, I don't need to be protected?"

He chuckled. "Sure, say it," he said. "I can agree with you."

She turned and looked over at him. "Then why did you tell Kevin you could see ghosts?"

"It seemed like the thing to do at the time," he said. "I don't think it had anything to do with protecting you, just deflecting."

She smiled. "Bradley, deflecting is another word for protecting."

"Not in my dictionary. Mary, when I left to get dinner, what did you and Kevin talk about?"

"Once you walked away I could see ghosts again," she said. "I saw the cop...and you are going to have to explain how you did that. But I saw a young girl standing behind Kevin. I guess I was...worried, so I asked him about his cases."

"Okay, I saw her too," he said. "What did he tell you?"

"First, how did you see her?"

"When you and I make contact, I can see ghosts, right?" he asked.

She nodded.

"Okay, well, even though I'm clearing them off the radar for you, I can still see them," he said. "It's really weird, like movies superimposed on each other."

"Yeah, that's what I see," she said. "So, you actually saw that cop..."

"And the girl," he said. "I saw her at your parent's place, at the Martins and then again at the restaurant. She seemed connected to Kevin."

"Yes, he told me he was working on a case, trying to save her," Mary explained. "He said he

114

thought she might have developed a crush on him. Then she disappeared. He is presuming she's dead."

"Well, he's right," Bradley said solemnly. "She looks pretty bad."

"I told him that you might be able to help him," she added. "I hope you don't mind."

No problem as long as he keeps his hands off of you.

"No, problem," he said, "a friend of yours is a friend of mine."

In a pig's eye, Bradley growled silently.

"Thanks! Maybe after we find Jeremy we can help him," she said, yawning. "I think I need to get some sleep."

"Yeah, tomorrow is going to be a busy day."

She walked to her bedroom door and turned to him. "Thanks for coming with me," she said. "You've made a big difference. I'm lucky to have you as a friend."

"Mary," he started.

What can I say? I want to be more than friends, but I'm married. Yeah, that would sound brilliant.

"Yes?" she asked, pausing by her bedroom door.

"Sweet dreams."

He sat back on the chair and stared out the window into the sky over Lake Michigan. Things were getting more complicated with each moment he spent with her. A couple of months ago he thought she was completely nuts, and now he was seeing ghosts too. What happened to his quiet, self-absorbed world? He chuckled softly, *Mary happened.*

He got up and walked over to his bedroom, picked up a couple of pillows and a blanket and carried them back to the couch. Placing the pillows on one end, he threw the blanket along the length of the couch. Glancing over to Mary's closed bedroom door, he nodded. *Close enough to keep her safe tonight.*

In the time it took him to wash up and change into sweats, something had changed in the layout of the make-do bed. A large depression had appeared in the middle of the couch. Bradley moved closer and sniffed.

"Oh, no, you don't," he said. "I am not sharing my bed with a dog, ghost or not. Off!"

The depression disappeared.

"Good boy," Bradley said. "You might as well take my bed; no one is going to use it."

Bradley glanced through the open door in his bedroom and saw a depression appear on the remaining comforter. "Smart dog."

He lay down on the couch, his eyes turned toward Mary's door and hoped for at least a little sleep that night.

Mary was dreaming she was on a boat in a lake, the waves lapping up against the side, rolling gently up and down in the water.

"Come on, baby," a man's breathless voice panted urgently, "we're almost there. Gotta hurry so Al don't miss us."

"Take it easy, Sonny," a woman's petulant voice responded. "I ain't no racehorse."

Mary slowly turned her head and opened her eyes. Platinum blonde hair shared her pillow. Looking up she saw the flaccid naked man looming above her, his forehead covered in sweat. He looked down at Mary and smiled. "You want a turn, baby?"

Mary rolled out of bed and hit the floor with a loud thump. Scooting backward across the room, she heard the shrill laughter of the two ghosts echo in her ears. When she hit the wall, she jumped up and bolted toward the door. She wrenched the door open and ran straight into Bradley, who had woken immediately when he heard the thump from her room.

Bradley caught Mary to him, and moved to shelter her from whatever had frightened her. With Mary in his arms, he had a complete view of what was going on in her room. He couldn't help himself; he laughed.

"It's not funny," Mary punched him, her head still buried in his chest.

"No, of course, not," he said, still peering into the room. "It's more disturbing than anything else."

"Bradley, stop watching, that's disgusting," she said.

He shrugged. "It's kind of like a train wreck," he said. "You can't help yourself."

Suddenly Mary's bedroom was riddled with the sound of Tommy-gun fire.

"Well, now we know why they're still here," Bradley said, guiding Mary over to the couch. "You sit here and I'll close the door."

He walked over to the bedroom door. Without Mary's touch, all he saw was a hotel room with a slightly mussed bed. He was glad he didn't have to view the bullet-riddled bodies of the lovers. Pulling the door closed, he turned and saw Mary sitting in the corner of the couch, her arms wrapped around her body.

He grabbed his blanket and placed it around her, pulling her gently into his arms. "Sorry," he said, "not very sensitive of me to laugh. It must have been frightening to wake up with those two sharing your bed."

Mary nodded. "I was dreaming I was in a boat on a lake, rocking gently on the waves."

Bradley turned his head away.

"Are you laughing at me?" Mary demanded.

"Sweetheart, I am trying my best not to laugh," he confessed.

"Yeah, it was real funny when he asked me if I wanted a turn."

"He said what?" Bradley growled, he turned her to face him. "I thought they couldn't connect if you didn't respond to them."

Mary shook her head. "They can't connect to me," she said. "But they can see me and they can try to interact. They were very much aware I was in that room with them."

He tightened his hold around her. "Okay, we are quickly changing from funny to creepy," he said. "How are you doing now?"

She yawned. "Better, thanks."

She looked around the room, finally putting two and two together. "Why are you sleeping on the couch?"

He shrugged. "The dog wanted the bed," he said.

"He can have mine," she said, grinning.

"Can ghost dogs bite ghost people?"

"I'm willing to give it a shot."

"I have a better idea," he said, grabbing one of the pillows and placing it on the arm of the couch where they sat. "You rest here for a while, then we'll figure out the rest."

Too tired from several nights of no sleep to argue, Mary let Bradley lower her head to the pillow and stretched out along the couch, still held in his arms. "Why are you still holding me?"

"So, I can keep the bad guys away," he replied.

"But how will you sleep?" she asked with a yawn.

He lifted his feet onto the coffee table in front of him. "Don't worry," he whispered. "I've slept in far worse positions than this."

A few minutes later, her even breathing told Bradley she had finally succumbed to sleep. He looked down at her and tenderly pushed her hair from her face. "Ahhh, Mary, what are we going to do with each other?"

"Woof."

Looking over, he saw the Golden Retriever standing next to the couch, wagging its tail and eager for fun.

"Do you want to play, fella?" Bradley whispered.

The dog stretched his forepaws in front of him and wagged his tail harder. "Good boy," he said. "Go get the ghosts in Mary's room. Sic 'em boy!"

The dog cocked its head to the side for a moment, then grinned, his tongue lolling out of the side of his mouth and darted through the door into Mary's room. The sounds of several ghosts yelling and a dog barking were music to his ears. "Good dog," he whispered, before sliding down on the couch, pulling Mary closer and falling asleep himself.

Chapter Sixteen

A sharp knock on their hotel room door had Bradley rushing from the bathroom to open it before Mary woke up. With only a towel slung around his waist, he pulled the door open to see Sean standing in the doorway.

"What the hell are you doing running around half-naked with my sister in the suite?" Sean asked.

"Quiet, she's still sleeping," he said. "And if you hadn't pounded on the door like a jackhammer, I might be a little more presentable."

Sean walked in and looked around the suite. Through the open door to Bradley's room he could see the blankets and pillows had been stripped off. Glancing at the couch, he saw the missing items and his sister, snuggled up in them.

"You playing sleep-over with my sister?" he growled.

Bradley rolled his eyes and worked to control his temper.

"Listen, big brother, you picked the most haunted hotel in Chicago for your sister to stay in, knowing damn well that she would be able to see what happened to make them ghosts," he said. "Would you like to sleep in a bed with two people shot to death by a Tommy-gun?"

Sean leaned back against the door, his face white. "Damn, I didn't think," he said. "I didn't realize that she could see...I only thought she could..."

"Yeah, well, she's fine. She slept," Bradley said, "but she had a rough night, so I thought she could sleep in for a while."

Sean nodded. "Good idea," he said. "Thanks for taking care of her. I appreciate it."

Bradley glared at Sean. "I don't give a damn what you appreciate. I take care of Mary because I want to."

Bradley walked away and closed his bedroom door behind him. He didn't know who he was angrier with, Sean or himself. Sean should have never placed Mary in this kind of situation. And he needed to put some space between himself and Mary. He couldn't have feelings for Mary until he knew whether Jeannine was alive or not. He leaned against the dresser and closed his eyes. *Be honest, Bradley,* he thought, *you already have feelings for her, and now you're going to have to figure out what to do about them.*

Mary woke slowly, her eyes adjusting to the brightness of the room. It took a moment for her to remember where she was and what she'd been doing when she fell asleep.

Bradley.

How do you walk that fine line between admiration and friendship, and love?

She rubbed her hand over her heart. Damn, she'd crossed the line.

She sighed. He wasn't ready to love again; his heart was still attached to Jeannine. *Well, crap, another secret I'll have to keep to myself.*

She sat up and stretched.

"Hey, sleepyhead, 'bout time you woke up," Sean's voice rang across the room.

She turned; disappointed it wasn't Bradley greeting her.

"Well, we had a little excitement last night," she said. "So, I suppose Bradley let me sleep in."

Sean nodded. "Yeah, he told me about it," he said.

Everything? Mary wondered.

"I'm sorry Mary, I wasn't thinking when I booked you into this hotel," he said, walking across the room and sitting on the back of the couch. "I didn't realize you could see how people became ghosts." He shrugged. "I guess I wasn't thinking at all," he continued. "Seeing two people murdered in your bed must have been frightening."

Not everything. Mary breathed a sigh of relief.

"Actually, Bradley got me out of there just before the gun fight," she said, "so I didn't have to see the worst of it."

"I don't know, I think what you saw was pretty frightening," Bradley said, slyly winking at her as he walked over to the small kitchenette and pulled a diet soda out of the refrigerator. "Breakfast?"

She grinned. "Yes, thank you," she answered. "How did you sleep?"

He twisted the cap off the bottle and brought it over to her. "Best sleep I've had in ages," he said, "except for some incessant snoring that I'm assuming must have been supernatural."

She blushed. "Snoring?"

"Could have woke the dead," he teased. "As a matter of fact, I think it did."

He cocked his head toward Mary's bedroom. "Your new pet cleared the room last night and promptly made himself comfortable on your bed," he said, sending her a teasing smile. "What? Did you think I meant you?"

She shook her head and stood up. "You are such a jerk," she said with a chuckle. "I'm going to go get dressed."

Once she closed the door behind her, Sean turned to Bradley. "Does she know about your wife?"

Bradley walked back to the kitchenette and pulled out another diet soda, opened it and took a swig before he felt calm enough to answer Sean. "Look, I understand you're her big brother," he said, "but where do you get off investigating my background?"

Sean shrugged. "She's my sister who died in my arms," he said, "on a stake-out I sanctioned, taking a bullet meant for me. That's where I get off."

Bradley dropped into the nearest seat. "Wow. Okay, she didn't tell me that part," he said.

Sean shook his head. "She never does," he said. "She just says she got shot, wrong place, wrong time."

Bradley nodded.

"Well, if you throw yourself between a gunman and your brother, it's not really considered wrong place, wrong time," he said softly. "It's called…"

His voice cracked.

"It's called giving everything for the people you love," Bradley said.

Sean nodded, unable to speak.

"She knows about Jeannine," Bradley said. "She knows as much as I do. I told her on the way in."

"Thanks," Sean said. "Does she know you love her?"

Bradley stood up. "That's none of your damn business."

Sean grinned. "Yeah, but you answered my question," he said. "Take care of her. She may not look like it, but she has a tender heart."

"I will do everything in my power to make sure she is never hurt," Bradley said, "which might entail never letting this relationship go beyond friendship."

"I suppose that's good enough for now," Sean said, standing and offering Bradley his hand.

Chapter Seventeen

"Okay, you are supposed to look like a devoted husband and a man who is looking forward to becoming a father," Mary explained, her breath coming out in puffs of steam as they walked down Michigan Avenue in the sub-freezing weather. "Not like a bad-ass cop who is going to rush in and save the day."

"But I am a bad-ass cop who's going to rush in and save the day," Bradley responded with a grin. "Besides, wouldn't Josh be a little skeptical?"

Mary nodded. "Yes, a little," she said. "But he wouldn't let it show too much for Abby's sake."

"Okay, so I'm slightly skeptical, but willing to forgo that for the woman I love?" he asked.

"Pretty much," Mary said. "Think you can handle it?"

Bradley stopped walking, turned to Mary and placed his hands on her upper arms. "You mean everything to me," he said softly, searching her eyes. "You are my heart, my soul and the reason I look forward to each day. You are simply the reason I live and breathe."

Mary swallowed, nodded her head and tried to quiet her wildly beating heart. "Okay, yes," she whispered. "You can handle it."

"Not done yet," Bradley said, pulling her closer.

He bent his head so their foreheads touched. "There is an elderly couple just getting out of a cab in front of the art museum," he said. "What do you think?"

Like I can think.

Mary peered around him and saw the couple. Then she saw Joey appearing next to them. "Joey just showed up," she whispered back. "I think we have our couple. The creeps."

Bradley smiled and rubbed his hands up and down Mary's arms, then pulled her close. Arms wrapped around her he bent his head and whispered into her ear, "Remember, you're a devoted wife who wants a baby, and not a bad-ass private investigator ready to kick some kidnapper butt."

Mary chuckled into his shoulder. "Shut up."

He laughed. "That's my girl."

They walked, hand in hand, into the museum, paying no attention to the elderly couple eyeing them. They stopped, a few feet away from the couple. Mary turned her face up to Bradley's and sent him a watery smile. "I can't believe we're going to meet our baby," she cried.

Bradley traced a finger gently across her cheek, wiping away a stray tear. "It's a happy day," he said, "you're not supposed to cry."

"Tears of joy," she said, raising up on her toes and brushing a soft kiss across his lips.

Bradley caught her and held her for a moment, exhaling slowly while he searched her face. "Let's go get our baby."

They walked up the massive marble stairs to the second floor and followed the signs to Gallery 240. They stood in front of the massive painting of a day in a French park, waiting for the elderly couple to make contact with them. They didn't have to wait long.

"Are you the Martins?" an elderly woman asked. Had Jeremy's mother been there, she would have recognized the woman as the helpful grandmother from the store.

Mary quickly turned around, smiled brightly. "Yes! Yes, I'm Abby Martins and this is my husband, Josh. Are you from the agency?"

The woman nodded. "Yes, dear, we just have a few more papers to sign and details to go over."

Mary looked around the gallery. "But where is the baby?" she asked. "I thought we would be getting the baby today."

The woman shook her head. "No need to worry, my dear," she said. "Since the weather was so brutal and we still had these last details to attend to, we thought it best not to bring the baby out. As soon as we take care of these things, we'll bring you the baby."

Mary let her eyes fill with tears and she clasped Bradley's hand, turning her face into his shoulder. "It's okay, darling," he said, "I'm sure it's just a formality."

He turned to the woman. "Is there a problem? Because if there is, I wish you had told us about it yesterday when we were on the phone with you," he said. "This is really hard on my wife."

The woman smiled. "Oh, no. No problem," she said. "You're exactly right, merely a formality. Now, our records show we never received the $10,000 processing fee. Do you know if that was paid?"

Bradley shook his head. "I never heard about a processing fee," he said.

"Oh, dear, I don't know how that could have happened," the woman said, shaking her head. "You didn't receive the letter requesting the fee?"

Mary turned back and shook her head. "No, we didn't," she said. "Oh, is that a problem?"

The woman smiled sweetly, but Mary could see the avarice in her eyes. "Well, my dear, normally it would mean the baby should go to the next family on the list," she explained.

Mary crumpled against Bradley and he folded her into his arms.

"Listen, I can write you a check right now," he said urgently. "We have to have this baby. Abby has waited too long for this to happen."

The woman nodded. "Well, I'm not supposed to do this," she said. "But you seem like such a nice couple. Yes, if you can write me the check today, written on a local bank, we can get the baby to you this afternoon."

Bradley nodded and pulled out the checkbook Sean had provided for them. The checkbook fell from his hands onto the floor next to the woman. She smiled and picked it up, handing it back to Bradley.

He smiled and nodded. "Thanks, I appreciate it."

He opened the book and wrote the check, taking care not to touch the checkbook where she had. "There," he said, handing it to her. "Is there anything else you need from us?"

The woman pulled out a few forms and requested their signatures, explaining the forms would be filed with the Secretary of State to insure the baby was legally theirs. Both Bradley and Mary filled out the forms as the Martins. In a few moments, the transaction was over.

"Once we have verified funds for your check, I'll call and let you know where we can meet," she said. "Do you have any questions?"

"Oh," Mary gushed. "I brought a gift for him. Could you give it to him, from us?"

She pulled out a plush teddy-bear and handed it to the woman.

"That was very thoughtful," the woman said, placing the stuffed animal in her bag. "I know he will love it. I'll be in touch."

She turned and walked out of the room. Mary once again turned herself into Bradley's arms and was held close. "I wanted to scratch her eyes out," Mary muttered.

Bradley laid his head on top of Mary's. "That's the kick-ass private investigator we all know and love," he chuckled. "I was getting worried."

"That I was going soft?" she asked.

"No, that you were going to lose it and take her out."

She laughed softly. "Yeah, well thanks for letting me take out my frustrations on you," she said. "Did I hurt you when I squeezed your arm?"

"I'll never play the violin again," he shrugged.

She looked up at him and raised one eyebrow. "But you never played it before, right?" she said.

He winked. "Caught me."

He looked over her shoulder, through the open doorway and at the lobby one story below. "Looks like they are leaving," he said, "but we should stand here for a few more minutes, just in case."

"In case of what?" Mary asked, placing her head against his shoulder enjoying the solid strength of it.

In case I never get another reason to hold you like this, Bradley thought.

"In case they come back," he said, tightening his hold on her.

"You two done hugging?" Joey asked.

Bradley looked over Mary's shoulder to Joey and replied, "No, I'm not. Go away."

Joey grinned. "I know you're just teasing me, Chief Alden. So are we going to get Jeremy now?"

131

Mary regretfully slid out of Bradley's arms and turned to Joey. "Well, we want to do this carefully so they still think we want Jeremy," she said. "But we put a tracking device in a toy I gave her for Jeremy, so the police know where they are going."

Joey smiled. "So, the police are going to crash in the door and grab Jeremy?"

Bradley, his hand on Mary's shoulder, shook his head. "No, we want to catch all of the people who did this to Jeremy and to all of the other babies," he said. "So we are going to watch their apartment and see who else is involved."

"But we should have Jeremy safely delivered to us this afternoon," Mary added, "and then we can bring him back home to your mom."

Joey smiled. "I knew you could do it," he said. "I knew you would save Jeremy."

"Well, he isn't safe yet," Bradley cautioned. "So we need you to stay close and let us know if anything changes. Okay?"

"Okay, I'll let you know," he said, then faded away.

"I love that little boy," Mary said, rubbing a real tear from her face.

"Careful," Bradley said. "You're ruining your kick-ass reputation."

She laughed. "I think my secret is safe with you."

"Always," he said, placing his arm over her shoulders and guiding her out of the gallery. "Always."

Chapter Eighteen

Sean met them at the hotel room. "It looks like everything is going as planned," he said. "The GPS device is working fine. They are heading toward the River North District."

"Great," Mary said, offering Sean a soft drink from the refrigerator. "Now all we have to do is wait for the call and pick up Jeremy."

"I feel like I'm in an episode on television," Bradley said. "Nothing happens this fast in real life. It can take years to recover stolen infants."

"Yes, it really helps when you have a guardian angel giving you information," she said.

"Well, this is by no means over," Sean said. "We've set a trace with the check you wrote back to any account they might use. We've got undercover officers located around the area, waiting for our signal. And we're running the fingerprints we lifted from the checkbook to see if she has a record and any known accomplices."

"You guys are right on top of things," Bradley said.

"Thanks for your help on this, Sean," Mary added.

He shrugged. "Hey, no big deal," he said. "These creeps have slipped through our fingers enough times. If not for you and Joey, we wouldn't be this close."

They gathered around the sitting area, eating the lunch Sean provided, and waiting for the phone call from the Martins. "Where's Kevin?" Mary asked.

"He's at the station," Sean said. "I've got his cell, so when this goes down, he can be there."

Mary nodded and was about to speak when she caught something out of the corner of her eye. She reached over and grabbed Bradley's hand. "Joey's back."

"Something's wrong," Joey cried. "Something's really wrong. They're gonna kill my brother."

"Joey, tell us what happened," Bradley said.

"They got a phone call and then they started screaming about a set-up," he said. "They are packing up all their stuff."

Mary turned to Sean. "The perps know they didn't meet with the Martins. They are pulling out and are talking about killing Jeremy."

"Okay, I'll get my guys to close in," he said, lifting his walkie-talkie and immediately connecting to the officers. "I want all patrols to close in now."

He jumped up. "Come on, my car's downstairs. We've tracked them to Kingsbury and Grand Avenue – that's less than two miles away."

Bradley and Mary grabbed their coats and ran after Sean. The squad car was parked at the curb; they jumped in and flew through traffic. As they neared their destination, Mary and Bradley watched out the windows for any sign of the couple while Sean maneuvered through the traffic. They barreled down Canal Street and turned onto the Grand Avenue Bridge. "Damn, I see them," Bradley called. "Stop the car!"

Sean screeched to a halt, but Bradley was already jumping out of the squad car and racing down the stairs to the river walk below. Mary jumped out after him, her heart in her throat. It was clear they were planning to throw Jeremy into the freezing waters of the Chicago River.

Bradley took the stairs four at a time, his eyes fixed on the elderly couple fifty yards away who moved with determination toward the bank. Jeremy was screaming at the top of his lungs, which only made the couple more anxious to get rid of him.

"Stop! Police!" Bradley called, hoping they would drop Jeremy and run.

The man took the crying baby out of the woman's arms, ran to the edge of the embankment and threw the baby into the choppy, freezing water. The couple turned and ran the other way. Bradley threw off his coat and dove into the river after the baby.

The freezing water hit his chest like a solid wall of ice. He lost his breath for a moment, but inhaled deeply and pressed on in the water. He could see the blue blanket bobbing up and down on the waves, but it was being carried downstream faster than he could swim. He felt his body begin to react to the cold, but he had no choice but to go on.

Suddenly, the baby stopped moving downstream, as if it were caught on something. Bradley allowed the current to pull him toward the baby and within moments, he had pulled the baby into his arms. He took a deep breath, willing his body to move before hypothermia set further in, and pulled himself with one arm toward the bank.

Mary ran along the embankment carrying a life preserver she had pulled from one of the boxes along the river. "Bradley, I'm here," she called, climbing down the metal casings to an old wooden dock extending into the river. "Just a few more feet!"

She leaned as far as she could and threw the life preserver toward them. Bradley grabbed it and secured his arm through it. "Mary," he gasped, "I don't have much more strength."

"Just hold on and enjoy the ride," she said, pulling against the current with all of her might, "just a few more seconds."

She pulled him alongside the dock and secured the rope to an old piling. She reached down; the water level was two feet below the dock. "I can't pull you both up by myself," she said.

"Mary, take the baby," Bradley gasped. "Then I can hold on with both hands until help comes."

She reached down and grabbed the edges of the blanket and pulled Jeremy up on the dock. The baby was stiff and unresponsive. She unwrapped the baby from the blanket and wet clothes, opened her coat and enclosed his tiny frame next her body beneath her coat.

"Sean will be here in a moment," she said, shivering in the cold. "He's called for paramedics. We'll get you out of there. Just hold on."

"I want...a hot...bath," Bradley stammered, his teeth chattering.

Mary nodded, tears filling her eyes. "I'll be sure you get one, in a Jacuzzi tub."

He nodded and closed his eyes.

"Bradley," Mary screamed. "Don't you dare close your eyes! You stay awake, do you hear me?"

Bradley opened his eyes. "Yes...ma'am," he stuttered. "Mary... Tell them...to hurry."

Mary could hear the sirens above them on the street level. She heard Sean's voice calling to them to hurry and heard the rush of paramedics running across the pavement.

"They're here," she said. "Hold on for just another moment."

She waited until the paramedics were at the dock. "Ma'am, I don't know if this dock is going to hold all of our weight combined," the first one called to her. "Why you don't you bring the baby over here, and we'll come down and get your friend."

She turned to Bradley. "I'll be waiting for you on the dock," she said. "Keep holding on."

He nodded and Mary could see that he was too weak to do anything else. She ran to the edge of the dock, handing the baby up to another paramedic. She started to climb back up to the embankment when she heard the shot.

She screamed.

Bradley looked at her with astonishment as his shoulder blossomed in bright red blood. His head fell back, his arms slipped out of the life preserver and he floated downstream.

Chapter Nineteen

He watched as he floated away from the dock.

I'm going to die.

He saw Mary run back to the edge of the dock, pointing to him.

Mary. Damn, I never had a chance to kiss her.

He tried to focus, but his eyesight was getting blurry.

I can't kiss Mary; I have to find Jeannine first.

Jeannine? Was that Jeannine standing next to Mary on the dock? He tried to shake his head to clear it, but couldn't.

I'm hallucinating.

I wonder if you always hallucinate before you die. I'll have to ask one of Mary's friends.

Crap, maybe I'll end up being one of Mary's friends.

He could barely keep his eyes open and his shoulder hurt like hell. This was not the way it was supposed to end. He suddenly realized that he wasn't moving downstream any longer and his head was staying above water.

Wow, I've got powers that I haven't even begun to tap. Must be mind over matter.

Then he smelled it – wet dog.

No, really? The dog is saving me? Good dog!

He recognized the pull on his shirt was not the drag of the water. The ghost dog had him by the collar and was saving his life. He remembered how Jeremy had stopped in the middle of the river too.

Damn, this is a great dog!

Over the crests of the waves, he could see a bunch of emergency guys in an inflatable raft coming toward him. As long as the dog's jaws held, he'd be getting a second chance. He tried to wave to them, but his arms weren't working. Actually, nothing seemed to be working. Even his eyes seemed to be getting a little blurry.

Please dog, hold on.

Then there was darkness.

# # # #

Beep...beep...beep...beep.

The incessant tone of the monitor seemed to mesh with Mary's heartbeat. Sitting in a chair next to the bed where his unconscious body lay in the ICU at Northwestern Memorial Hospital, she tightened her grip on Bradley's limp hand. The warming blankets left his shoulders, head and arms exposed; the purple and brown bruising setting off the stark white of the bandage on his right shoulder. She lifted his hand to her lips and pressed a kiss on his palm.

The door opened and Sean walked in. He looked exhausted. The past twenty-four hours since they pulled Bradley from the river had not been easy on any of them.

"How's he doing?" he asked, leaning against the doorway.

Mary shrugged and she fought the tears filling her eyes. "No change," she said. "The doctor said that the bullet wound was clean, it didn't hit any internal organs or bones. And the...the hypothermia actually helped because...because there was less blood."

Sean nodded.

"They're worried about infection, of course, because...it is the Chicago River," she added, shuddering with each statement. "And they don't know...they're not sure...with his heart beat slowed for so long..."

She lifted his hand back up to her lips and held it there for a moment, oblivious to the tears streaming down her face. "We won't know about brain damage until he wakes up," she finished.

Sean walked across the room and put his arms around his sister. "He's strong," he said. "He's going to be fine."

Mary nodded through her tears. "Yeah," she sniffed. "He has to be."

"I know how much you hate hospitals. Do you want me to watch him for a while so you can take a break?"

Mary shook her head. "No, I have to be here. In case..."

Sean hugged her. "Don't you think he'd find you and say goodbye, no matter where you were? Not that I believe he's going to die."

Mary nodded. "Yes, he would, if he could," she said, "but I still have to be here."

"Hey, Bradley, don't you think you've spent enough time lying around?" he asked. "There's a family in pediatrics that wants to meet the man that saved Jeremy's life."

He leaned forward over the bed.

"What's that you said? Yeah, I know he was mostly saved because of my amazing driving ability," he continued, "but, being the modest fellow I am, I had to share the credit with you."

Mary smiled weakly. "Well, that was big of you, Sean," she said. "Bradley, you really have to get up and stop him from taking all the credit."

Sean smiled at her. "Jeremy is responding well to the treatment," he said. "Another mixed blessing; the cold water prevented him from drowning."

"It's a strange world we live in," Mary said. "You never know where a blessing will come from."

Sean nodded. "We don't have any leads on the shooter yet," he said. "The bullet could have come from anywhere."

"Hey, how's the big guy doing?" Kevin asked as he entered the hospital room.

"It's still too early to tell," Mary said.

"Well, let him know that we caught the couple and they are singing like canaries over at the station," he said. "They don't want to be tied to a cop's death."

Mary gasped.

"Oh, Mary, sorry," he said. "Listen, he's not going to die. He's going to be fine. Really."

She nodded and wiped her face with a tissue.

"Hey, listen, how about you let Sean watch over the psychic and I'll take you to get something to eat," he offered.

"That's okay," she said. "I need to stay here."

She looked up and saw the young girl still hovering behind Kevin. Obviously Bradley didn't chase away ghosts when he was unconscious.

"Are you sure?" Kevin pushed. "Really, you need to take care of yourself."

"Hey, Kevin, why don't we get back to the station and see if we can't find the guy who shot Bradley," Sean interrupted. "That'll make Mary feel better than a cheeseburger from the Billy Goat." He turned to Mary and whispered, "Now, at least try and sleep while you watch over your man."

"Thanks, Sean," she said. "Let me know if there are any more updates."

He kissed her on the top of her head. "I promise," he said.

As soon as the door closed behind them, Mary bent her head and leaned it against the mattress. "Dear Heavenly Father," she prayed, "I know you have a better view of things from where you are and I'm praying Bradley getting better is part of your plan. If it's not, could you please consider altering your plan a bit? I need him, Father. I know this is a selfish prayer, but it's from deep in my heart. Please, Father, please. Amen."

She wiped the tears from her eyes and took a deep breath. Sean was right, she needed to get a little sleep or she'd be no good to anyone. She looked around the room; anyplace that looked comfortable was too far away. She looked at Bradley lying motionless on the bed and made up her mind. She slipped onto the side of the bed, placed her head on his good shoulder and laid his arm around her. She pulled the extra blanket over both of them, hugged him to her and closed her eyes.

She woke a little while later. The lights from the hall were dimmed and the only light in the room was shining from the monitor next to the bed. Something had disturbed her. She lifted her head and scanned the room. A woman was standing just inside the door staring at them. Mary could see the door through the translucent figure. "Can I help you?" she asked.

The ghost met her eyes with a sad smile, placed her finger over her lips, as if to shush Mary, and faded into the night.

She laid her head back on Bradley's shoulder and started to close her eyes when she felt his arm tighten around her. "Why is it that whenever I work a case with you, I end up getting shot?" he asked, his voice dry and hoarse.

Joy and relief coursed through her. She turned her head to look at him. His eyes were clear and he was smiling down at her. "Just lucky, I guess," she responded, tears running down her face.

"Careful with those tears," he admonished lightly. "If this warming blanket is electric, you could shock us both."

She smiled. "Welcome back, Bradley."

"Back? Hell, I was just taking a well-deserved nap," he said.

Chapter Twenty

"Who shot me?" Bradley was sitting up against the back of the hospital bed, two days after he woke from his coma. He was feeling like his old self and he wanted answers. His question was directed to Sean, who sat in a chair next to Mary.

"I have no idea," Sean said. "It could have been anyone."

"When there's a shooting, there's generally a motive," Mary said. "We have to consider motive."

Kevin, standing against the door jamb, straightened and shrugged. "Could have been the kidnappers' accomplice," he suggested. "He was probably pissed you messed up his gig."

Mary shook her head. "If that was the case, I should have been the one who was shot," she said. "Standing on the dock I made a much better target than Bradley."

"Got any enemies?" Sean asked.

Bradley thought about it for a moment, shrugged and winced. His neck and shoulder still hurt like hell. "I can think of about a dozen people who aren't really happy with me," he said. "Maybe six who'd like to see me dead. But they're better shots than whoever did this."

Sean laughed. "Okay, I'll keep that in mind," he said. "Any residuals from the case last month?"

Mary shook her head. "No, we got the bad guy and he's in prison right now, awaiting a trial."

"Okay, prison," Bradley said, "just before we left I got a call that a fellow I put away for a while got out and he still held a grudge. But he'd be looking for me in DeKalb – not Freeport or Chicago."

"And there's your friend from the hotel lobby," Mary reminded him.

"You think Lily shot me?" he asked.

She rolled her eyes. "No, but Eddie Batolli might have found out you were in town."

"Batolli?" Sean asked. "Why is he gunning for you?"

Bradley started to shrug and thought better of it. "I put him away when he was a tough kid punk," he said. "He hasn't forgiven me either."

"So, who haven't you pissed off?" Kevin asked, rolling his eyes. "Look, maybe it was just a random kook deciding he wanted to shoot the guy in the river. Maybe that's all there is to it."

Bradley nodded. "I've got to say that makes the most sense," he agreed. "I think it was purely random. I just got caught in the wrong place at the wrong time."

Sean turned sharply and met Bradley's eyes. "There is no such thing."

Bradley nodded. "Yeah, well, maybe this time there is. And I'm a little tired of sitting on my butt in a hospital bed."

"You're forgetting that someone called the kidnappers and let them know it was a set up," Mary said. "Who would have had that kind of information?"

"Anyone working on the case," Sean said. "Damn, I hate having to suspect one of my guys."

"It doesn't have to be someone on the force," Kevin said. "Someone could have been keeping an eye on the Martins and figured us out."

Bradley nodded. "Yeah, that's a possibility, too. And I'm not helping anyone by sitting here in the hospital."

"The doctor wanted to monitor you," Mary said. "He said your body received quite a lot of trauma and they need to be sure you are fully recovered."

"I know exactly what my body went through; I was there," he argued, "and I'm feeling fine now."

Sean put his hands on his hips and shook his head. "No, I don't think that's a good idea. Not until we can either confirm the shooting was random or get a better idea of who we are dealing with. Get comfortable, Alden."

"You realize you're not my commanding officer," Bradley responded.

"You realize I can arrest you," Sean countered.

"For what?"

"It's illegal to go diving in the Chicago River," he smirked. "Stay put, Alden. Mary, come out to the hall with me, I've got to talk with you."

Kevin walked closer to the bed after Sean and Mary left the room. "I did a little checking on you," he said. "Sorry about your wife, that must have been hard."

Bradley stiffened. "Why the hell did you think checking up on me was a good thing to do?"

He put his foot on one of the chairs and leaned forward. "Mary is like the kid sister I never had," he said. "Just looking out for her."

"Funny, you don't seem to be treating her like a kid sister."

Kevin laughed. "Yeah, you're right; I'm not feeling brotherly toward her at all. Maybe I wanted to check out the competition."

"And you're telling me this because…"

"Cut her loose, Alden," he said. "You're not ready to give up on your wife and you're stringing Mary along. What kind of life is that? She deserves more than being an afterthought."

"She's not an afterthought," Bradley growled.

Sean and Mary entered the room. "Just think about what I've said," Kevin said.

He moved back to the door. "I'm going to follow up on some leads," he said to Sean. "I'll be at the station."

He took Mary's hand and brought it to his lips. "Now that your friend is feeling better, how about dinner tonight? Just the two of us. I know a place…soft lights, good food and the best jazz in the city. "

Mary shook her head. "Sorry, Kevin, it sounds wonderful, but not tonight. Thanks."

She gently pulled her hand out of his grasp.

"Yeah, okay, maybe another time," he said.

"That'd be nice. Rain check."

Kevin nodded and walked out of the room.

"I hope I didn't hurt his feelings," she said.

"He'll get over it, I'm sure," Bradley said. "So what's up between the two of you?"

"We've got a plan," Sean said.

Chapter Twenty-one

"Are you really sure you are up to this?" Mary quietly asked Bradley as they moved down the hospital corridor to the freight elevator. "You're a little big for me to throw you over my shoulder and carry you back."

"As I recall, you've already done that," he said with a grin.

"Well, it was either that or our friendly neighborhood serial killer was going to do away with you then and there," she said. "Besides, it was only from the cab to the back of his pick-up. Only a couple of feet." She stopped moving and looked back at him. "How did you know about that? You were drugged."

He shrugged. "Occasionally I get a flash of memory about that episode. Some are more interesting than others."

She blushed. "Don't rely on drug-induced flashbacks, they can be faulty."

He chuckled softly. "Or highly...stimulating."

"Are we going to sneak you out or stand here in the hospital and chat?" she asked.

"Hey, you were the one who stopped," he said, raising his hands in surrender. "I'm just the innocent victim. I don't know why we just didn't sign me out the normal way."

"Sean thought if the leak was internal, it would be safer sneaking you out," she said.

They moved further down the hall, Bradley holding on to Mary's shoulder. "Well, crap," Bradley whispered.

"What?" Mary asked.

He sighed deeply. "The nice old guy in 204, Mr. Watermann, just walked by and waved goodbye to me," he said.

She looked around, confused. "Where?"

"He was a ghost. You couldn't see him because you're standing next to me," Bradley reminded her. "Damn, he was such a nice old guy."

"How did you meet him?" she asked, turning to him.

"I got bored this afternoon and started visiting the neighbors," he replied. "He served in World War II – he was amazing."

"Was he very sick?" Mary asked.

Bradley nodded. "Yeah, he was. And he missed his wife. She died three years ago."

He watched the ghost move slowly down the corridor past the nurses' station. Suddenly, the room alert started ringing. "Code Blue, Mr. Watermann's room," a nurse called.

Mary and Bradley hid in a doorway while the team rushed to Mr. Watermann's room. "Can they bring him back?" Bradley asked.

"Only if he really wants to come," Mary said. "But it sounds like he was ready to go."

He looked back down the corridor and saw Mr. Watermann, still taking his time walking slowly away. Then he saw another figure come forward. At first all he could see was a gray mist, but soon it took form and moved quickly toward Mr. Watermann. Bradley could see the smile on his face and watched as he spread his arms out and hugged the woman before him. They embraced and kissed, and with his arm around her shoulders, slowly continued down the darkened hallway.

"He's not coming back," he said, his throat a little tight. "He's where he belongs."

Mary smiled. "She came for him, right?"

He nodded. "How did you know?"

"True love lasts beyond death," she said simply.

They continued down the corridor and to the freight elevator. Mary leaned forward and punched in the key code, the large doors slid open. "How did you get that code?" Bradley asked.

"You don't want to know," Mary replied with a grin.

The doors closed and Bradley turned to Mary. "Yeah, I really do want to know."

Mary shrugged. "Well, the new security guard is young and single and very virile," she said with a sigh. "And you know what men like that want?"

"It had better be fifty bucks," he responded.

She grinned. "Nah, I got it for thirty. I told him I was undercover, showed him my old badge."

"Brilliant," he said.

The doors slid open and they walked out onto the loading docks behind the hospital into the freezing night air. They walked the half-block to Bradley's waiting car. Mary climbed into the driver's seat. She glanced over at Bradley's attire of a thick robe, hospital gown and boots. "First stop, the hotel room, so you can slip into something more comfortable."

"Good idea," he said, pulling the hem of the gown down over his knees, "I'm feeling a little exposed. "

She giggled. "Well, at least you have the legs to pull off an outfit like that."

"Shut up and drive," he growled.

In fifteen minutes they were parked at the hotel and scurrying up the back elevator.

Mary unlocked the door to the hotel room. Sean was sitting on the couch looking out the window. "We've got a bigger problem than we thought," he said without turning around.

"What happened?" Bradley asked.

Sean turned and faced them. "There was a Code Blue," he said.

Mary and Bradley nodded. "We were there when it happened," Mary said.

"Where were you?"

"We were sneaking out through the freight elevator about then," Bradley admitted. "Why?"

"Because while the nurses were involved in the Code Blue, someone was able to slip something into your IV, the one you should have been wearing," he said, "if you hadn't slipped out."

"What was in the IV?" Mary asked.

"We don't know yet," Sean said. "They have it at the lab and will call me with results."

"How could they tell?" Bradley asked.

"Dawn, one of the nurses we work with regularly, knew about the plan to sneak Bradley out," Sean said. "She was going to cause a diversion if anything went wrong. She went into his room and saw the IV levels were higher than they should have been. She checked for tampering. Not a very professional job. Once she detected the puncture mark in the line, she sealed the room and called us immediately."

Bradley sat down on the couch. "Well, we know one thing for sure," he said. "The shooting wasn't random."

Chapter Twenty-two

"It makes perfect sense," Mary argued. "We go back to Freeport. It's our turf. Anyone who doesn't belong will be found out quick enough."

"I don't like it," Bradley said.

"Because you're not staying and fighting?" she asked. "Because after you've been shot and nearly poisoned, you'd like to give them another chance?"

Bradley ran his hand through his hair. "I can see how you might think that," he said. "And in a way, maybe that is part of the motivation. But mostly it's because this is where the clues are, this is where everything happened and this is where we can find whoever wants me dead."

"I prefer letting Sean find him and not giving whoever another shot at you."

The ringing of Sean's cell phone ended the conversation. Both Mary and Bradley watched as Sean stood up and paced around the hotel room.

"Okay," he said. "That's it. That's all they found? Could it have been a mistake? Okay. You're sure. Well, I appreciate it. Thanks."

Sean hung up the phone and shook his head. "Maybe this all was a big coincidence after all," he said. "The lab said the only thing they found in the

IV that shouldn't have been there was penicillin. No one dies from penicillin."

Bradley took a deep breath. "They do if they are allergic to it," he said.

"You're allergic to penicillin?" Sean asked.

"Allergic enough that a small dose, administered intravenously, would have stopped my heart," he said. "So, they've got access to my medical records too."

Mary stood up and walked to the window. "This is crazy," she said. "Sean, Bradley was supposed to be in a secure area, with police officers guarding his room. How the hell did someone slip through?"

"I don't know, but I've already started an investigation."

"An investigation is not going to keep Bradley safe," she argued. "We need to find out who the leak is in your department and fix it."

"Hey, Mary, take it easy," Bradley said. "Sean's doing all he can…"

"Well, it's not good enough," she interrupted, "not nearly enough."

She turned away from them, staring sightlessly out the window.

"Mary, I'll figure this out," he said softly, picking up his coat from the back of the couch. "I won't let someone else take a bullet because of me."

Mary turned around quickly. "Sean, I didn't…"

The door closed on her words. Mary covered her mouth with her hand, tears filling her eyes. "I didn't mean…"

Bradley pushed himself up from the couch and walked over to Mary. He pulled her into her arms. "Yeah, he knows," he said. "He's just as frustrated as you are. He's doing all he can, Mary."

"Damn it," she sniffed. "This was not supposed to happen."

Bradley laid his cheek on Mary's head. "Yeah, I know. But life has a way of changing the rules when you least expect it."

She wiped the remnants of the tears off her face and took a deep breath. "Well, I certainly don't want to just sit around waiting for them to try again," Mary said. "Let's go kick some bad-guy ass!"

Bradley laughed and then winced at the pain. "Okay, I'm in a kicking-ass mood," he said. "But perhaps we should figure out what we want to do before we change into our superhero outfits."

Mary chuckled softly. She stepped back and he let her slide out of his arms. She gently placed her hand in the middle of his chest. "Okay, here's the deal," she said with a watery smile. "You get to change into your superhero costume if you promise you won't try to stop speeding bullets with your body. Okay?"

He laid one of his hands over the one she placed on his chest and cupped her cheek with the other one. "As long as I can still leap tall buildings in a single bound, I'm good."

A shaky laughed escaped her lips before she could stop it. She covered her mouth with her free hand, controlling her emotions and nodded at him. "Deal."

"Mary, I'm not going to die," he said firmly. "I have too much to live for."

She sniffed. "Well, if you even consider getting hurt again, I'll kick your butt," she said.

"Well, then, that settles that," he said with a grin. "Now, about that plan…"

Chapter Twenty-three

"No, we don't need to check out Kevin," Mary stated. "I've known him since he was eight, he's clean."

"So, what's the harm, then?" Bradley argued. "If he's clean, then no harm no foul. Besides, he's the only lead we can follow up with tonight."

She shook her head. "Why are we even considering him? This makes no sense."

"My spidey-sense tells me this guy is hiding something," he said. "Listen, if you were a bad cop who had some skeletons in your closet, the last thing you'd want is some psychic hanging around talking up the people you've offed."

"But Kevin isn't a bad cop," she said.

"Prove it."

"How?"

"Let's go chat with one of Kevin's old partners," Bradley said. "If nothing else, we'll get some deep dish pizza."

It was nearly eleven o'clock, but Pizzeria Uno was still busy.

"We need to sit in the corner booth," Bradley said.

"And how are we supposed to accomplish that?" Mary asked.

"Still got your old badge?" he asked with a smile.

She smiled. "I like the way you think."

Within fifteen minutes they were seated together on one side of the corner booth with soft drinks and a plate of assorted appetizers. "Do you see him yet?" Mary asked, her hand linked with his.

Bradley shook his head. "Not yet," he said, turning and casually looking around the room. "Wait. There he is, by the bar."

"Okay, I'll go talk with him and invite him back to the booth," Mary said.

As she walked from the booth to the bar, away from Bradley, the intimate pizzeria's clientele increased substantially, but these ghostly customers wouldn't be ordering food any longer. She saw the large, dark-haired policemen who had to be Kevin's former partner standing at the end of the bar, trying unsuccessfully to toss Beer Nuts into his mouth.

A few minutes later, Sergeant Jack Monroe, formerly of the Chicago Police Department, was seated across from them at the booth. "So, you're Sean's little sister," Jack asked in a larger-than-life voice. "Damn, you don't look a thing like him. Lucky you!"

Jack laughed at his own joke. "Get it, don't look a thing like him?"

Mary chuckled, "Yeah, I get it."

"So, did you know Kevin Brady?" Bradley asked.

Jack nodded enthusiastically. "Oh, yeah, Kev's a good boy. We were partners," he explained, "always had my back."

Mary turned and gave Bradley an "I-told-you-so" smile.

"So, how did you die?" Bradley asked, ignoring Mary.

"Dammed if I know," Jack said. "One minute I'm eating all-meat deep dish, the next minute I'm watching the paramedics carry my body out the door."

"Sean thought you might have had a heart condition," Mary suggested.

"Hell no," Jack said. "Just had a physical the week before. The doc said I was strong as an ox. Had a ticker that would go the distance. Genetic thing. My grandfather lived until he was one-hundred-and-four, big as me too."

"Wait," Bradley said. "You didn't have a heart condition?"

Jack shook his head. "No, like I said, strong as an ox."

"What did the coroner say?" Mary asked.

"Hmmmm, well, I don't believe there was ever an autopsy," Jack said, scratching his head. "Come to think of it, why wasn't there?"

Mary pulled out her cell phone and called Sean.

"Hey, Sean, I just have a random question. Remember the officer Bradley saw at Uno's? What did he die from again? Yeah, that's right, heart attack. Now I remember. So, how did you know it was a heart attack?"

Mary paused and closed her eyes. "Well, of course, he was Monroe's partner, he would have known about his heart. Yeah, makes sense. Thanks, Sean."

She turned to Bradley, her phone still on her ear and shook her head sadly.

"No, we were just deciding on dinner, that's all," she lied into the phone. "Thanks, Sean. Bye."

She hung up the phone and turned to Jack. "Why would Kevin tell them that you had a heart condition you were covering up?"

"He said that?" Jack asked incredulously. "That's crazy. He knew I had just gone for my check-up."

"Jack, are you, by any chance, allergic to penicillin?" Bradley asked.

Jack nodded his head. "Oh, yeah, that stuff could kill..." He stopped. "You know, now that you mention it, I was feeling a little woozy on the night I died. We stopped in here, got a couple of sodas and ordered dinner. Halfway through dinner I was feeling pretty sick, nauseous. Then, I guess I died."

"Did you leave the table at any time?" Mary asked.

"Sure, after we ordered the drinks I went to the john," he said. "Pretty much the routine."

"What do you drink?" Bradley asked.

"Coke," John said. "I love a cold glass of Coke."

"That could have masked the taste," Mary said. "And the allergic reaction would have started with nausea and then finally become a full blown anaphylaxis attack."

"So, you're saying someone killed me?" Jack asked. "You're saying Kevin killed me? Why the hell would he do something like that?"

"Well, that's the next big question," Bradley said. "What were you working on with Kevin at the time of your death?"

Jack pondered for a few minutes, and then his eyes filled up with tears. "I can't seem to remember," he said. "It seems so long ago."

"That's okay, Jack," Mary said. "It's hard to remember things like that. Things that you didn't think were important at the time."

"Jack, there was a young girl, she looked Hispanic, she used to be a prostitute," Bradley said.

"Yeah, little Maria Hernandez," Jack said. "Cute as a button. We got in touch with her parents and sent her home. She was a runaway who got mixed up with the wrong people."

"Jack, she never made it home," Mary said. "She died. Kevin said she was a prostitute who got caught up in a bad deal."

"No, no, we sent her home," he insisted. "I bought her an airplane ticket with my own money. She was supposed to go home."

"When?" Bradley asked.

Jack thought for a moment. "The day I died."

Chapter Twenty-four

"I can't believe this," Sean said, running his hand over his face. "You can't expect me to believe this. We've known Kev since he was a kid. He couldn't be a killer. He just couldn't."

"People change," Mary said. "And we haven't really kept up with Kevin for the past few years. I know you don't want to believe it."

Sean turned on Mary. "And you do?" he asked. "You want to believe it?"

Bradley walked between the two siblings. "Hey, if you want to get angry, get angry with me because I insisted we check it out," he said. "Or, better yet, get angry with Kevin, who not only betrayed your friendship, but killed a fellow cop."

Sean shook his head and walked across the room. "Yeah, yeah, you're right," he said. "It's just..."

"He was your friend," Bradley said, "and it would hurt the most to have someone you thought was a friend betray you."

Sean nodded. "Yeah, something like that," he said.

"We have to assume that it was Kevin who tipped off the kidnappers," Mary said, "and shot Bradley because he thought he could see ghosts."

"And it makes sense he would use penicillin again," Bradley said. "It worked for him last time."

"He just sat there and watched his partner die?" Sean asked, shaking his head. "What happened to him?"

Mary walked over and put her arms around her brother. "I don't know, Sean," she said. "But he's not the same person he was when we were little."

He nodded. "You're right, and now we need to bring him in," he said. "But we have to be smart about it; we need to get evidence in order to make this stick."

"I think I need to go on a date with Kevin," Mary said.

"No!" Bradley and Sean stated emphatically.

"Stop being such men," Mary said. "He doesn't know I can talk to ghosts. He doesn't know we know about Jack. And he thinks he's pulled one over on us."

"I'm going with," Bradley said.

"Stop! I am a trained police officer. I've done undercover. And if you come, you'll block me from seeing Maria," she said. "I appreciate your concern, but, really, this is the only way this can go down."

"I really don't like this," Sean said.

Mary smiled. "Yeah, you only say that when you know it's the only way," she said.

"Do you have any undercover cops Kevin wouldn't recognize?" Bradley asked Sean.

"No, they've all worked Vice," he said. "And even if he didn't know them, a cop can recognize another cop a mile away."

"Damn," Bradley ran his hand through his hair. "Isn't there another way?"

Mary shook her head. "No, he's done a really good job covering his tracks. Anyone who could have testified against him has ended up dead."

"You know, that wasn't the thing to say to make me feel any better about this," Bradley said, walking over to the window.

"Yeah, sorry," she said, and then turning to Sean added, "I'll call him first thing in the morning and set it up."

"Okay, I'll make sure there's back-up close by," Sean said. "Bradley, you want to ride with me?"

Bradley nodded, but didn't turn and face him. "Yeah, that'd be great, thanks."

Sean stood and walked to the door. "Oh, just so you know. Your bed was moved into a private room in intensive care because you had a near-fatal reaction to some misadministered penicillin. You're in a coma and not expected to survive."

"Well, that's the best news I've heard all day," Bradley said.

Sean nodded and left the hotel room.

The silence in the room was deafening. Bradley stood looking out into the night sky. Mary stood next to the couch her arms wrapped around herself.

"I guess I'll get ready for bed," she said finally. She walked slowly to her room.

"Mary," he said, still looking out the window. "You'll never get any sleep in there. We can share the couch again."

"But your shoulder..." she started.

He turned. The intensity in his eyes stopped her words.

I need to hold you tonight, Mary. Watch over you while you sleep.

"I'll be fine," he said.

She nodded. "Thanks, that'd be nice."

Chapter Twenty-five

Mary slowly opened her eyes. The sun had risen over the waters of Lake Michigan casting a dusty rose hue to the sky and gilding the blue waters with gold. The darkness of the hotel room was beginning to fade, replaced with warm light. She turned her head and gazed at Bradley's face, propped against the cushions of the couch above her. His hair was brushed forward on his forehead and his mouth was relaxed in a smile that Mary adored.

She lifted her hand to brush the hair back when a movement across the room caught her eye.

The woman stood close enough to the window that the morning rays of sun passed through her and onto the carpeted floor. Mary recognized her as the same woman she had seen at the hospital. Had she too been a victim of Kevin's actions?

"Can I help you?" Mary whispered.

The woman smiled sadly and, once again, lifted her finger to her lips and faded away.

No sooner had she left than Mary felt Bradley's arms tighten around her. She looked up and his eyes met hers.

"Hi," he whispered, "how did you sleep?"

"I've never slept better," she replied. "How are you? How's your shoulder?"

"What shoulder?" he asked with a smile.

"The one that probably hurts like hell about now," she said.

"Oh, that one. It hurts like hell."

Mary chuckled and sat up. "I'll get your meds."

She popped open the bottle of pain killers Sean had brought from the hospital and pulled a bottle of water from the refrigerator. "About last night," she began, as she walked back to him.

Bradley shook his head. "No, we really don't need to go there," he said. "You're right. I hate it, but you're right. The only way to catch him is to talk to Maria."

She smiled and passed him the pills and water. He swallowed them and then slowly stretched. "Yep, hurts like hell," he muttered.

She sat on the chair next to the couch. "And?" she asked.

"And what?"

"And what advice do you want to give me?" she asked with a smile.

He met her eyes with complete soberness. "Don't take risks. Don't do anything stupid. And if you get hurt, I'm going to kick your butt."

She nodded and dialed her cell phone. "Hey, Kevin, am I interrupting you?" she asked. "Oh, that's good. Hey, listen, can I redeem that rain check from the other night?"

She paused and listened for a moment.

"Yeah, I need to get away, think about something else," she said. "Bradley is in pretty bad shape, they don't think he's going to make it."

Her breath caught and tears filled her eyes. She sniffed. "Sorry, I'm a little emotional," she said. "Anyway, Sean is kicking me out of the hospital for a while to get some fresh air. I just wondered if we could do something.

"Yeah, that would be great," she said. "Do you want me to meet you there or do you want to pick me up?"

She nodded. "Okay, I'll be in the hotel lobby at eleven. Thanks, Kevin."

She hung up the phone and took a deep breath.

"Well, it's done."

Bradley shook his head. "No, it's just beginning. Where is he…?"

A knock on the hotel room door interrupted him. "Hey, it's Sean," he called from the other side of the door.

Mary got up and let him in. He was carrying a shopping bag from a local restaurant. "I thought I'd bring in breakfast," he said. "And then we could set things up."

He took a look around the room, noting the blankets piled on the couch and Bradley still stretched out on the couch. "Any problems last night?" he asked.

"None," Mary said. "I slept like a babe in arms."

Bradley coughed to cover his laughter.

"Something wrong?" Sean asked.

Bradley turned and looked directly at Sean.

"No, as a matter of fact, we're good," he said. "Mary just made contact with Kevin and she was about to give me the details. So your timing is perfect."

Sean brought the bag over, pulled out two bottles of diet cola and handed them to Bradley and Mary with a smile. "I'm nothing if not observant," he said.

"You're my hero," Mary said, taking a long drink.

"I second that," Bradley said, mirroring Mary's actions.

"Kevin's going to pick me up at eleven and we're going to a Mexican place out near Loyola University," she said. "Do you know the place?"

Sean nodded. "Yeah, I've been there with him. It's a family-owned place. A hole-in-the-wall, but the food is great, and at eleven it's not going to be very busy."

"Can we get access to the hotel room next door?" Bradley asked.

"Why? Kevin is going to pick me up in the lobby?"

"You said you'd meet him in the lobby at eleven," Bradley replied. "My guess is that he comes here, to the hotel room, at ten-thirty to get some alone time with you."

"Do you think he's plotting something?" Mary asked.

173

"Yeah, but it has nothing to do with murder," Bradley answered. "He's hoping to get lucky, Mary."

"Ohhhhhh," Mary said, blushing. "Wait, how would you know he'd do something like that?"

"Be very careful with how you answer that question," Sean advised.

Bradley grinned. "Mary, you are a beautiful woman and he's a ladies' man," he said. "Of course he's going to try and push you."

"Good answer," Sean whispered.

"Sean, I heard you," Mary replied.

"Yeah, I know," he grinned.

After Sean gained access to the room next door, they set up both listening devices and cameras throughout the suite. As Sean moved into Mary's bedroom with a camera Bradley stopped him. "You're not going to need one in there," he said.

Sean was confused. "Why not?"

"Because if he pulls her in there, I'm coming through the door, and it's all over."

Sean studied Bradley for a moment, saw the steely determination in his eyes, and nodded. "Okay."

By ten they were done getting the hotel room ready, just in case Bradley's intuition proved correct. Mary excused herself to get ready for her date.

"Where's your car?" Bradley asked.

"I have a rental today, no marks at all," Sean replied. "I've got a portable siren in case we need it, but I didn't want Kevin to spot us."

Bradley nodded. "Good. How many minutes do we wait before we follow?"

"I've got officers planted around the area," he said. "They will inform us once they get into Kevin's car. We also have cars situated along the route to confirm he brings her where he says he's going."

"Okay, good. How close can we get to the restaurant?"

Sean shook his head. "Not real close," he said. "That's a problem. The place is really small and tucked in under the L-tracks. I've got a couple cops who go in there regularly who will just happen to be there for lunch when Kevin walks in – but you and I are going to have to stay back."

"Will someone be in the next room once we leave, in case he brings her back up here?"

"My plan is that he doesn't get that chance," Sean said. "Mary will send me a text when she's received the information from Maria. Then I'll call her and tell her that you've taken a turn for the worse and she needs to get back to the hospital. I'll tell her I'm on my way to get her."

"I like that," Bradley said. "Get her away from him as soon as possible."

"Well, you might not like this. After this date, once Mary gets the information, I want you both out of Chicago," Sean said. "We'll handle the investigation."

"Yeah, you're right, I don't like it," Bradley agreed, "but I get it. I can have us on the road within thirty minutes."

"I'll have my guy in Freeport keep you up to speed," Sean said.

"Good, I want to meet your guy," Bradley said.

Sean laughed. "Yeah, I bet you do."

Mary stepped out of her room dressed in skinny jeans, a form-fitting black turtleneck and high-heeled half-boots. "Don't you have something, I don't know...looser, you could wear?" Sean asked.

"Yeah, like sweats," Bradley suggested. "You've always looked good in sweats."

Mary shook her head. "What are you talking about?" she asked. "I wear this all the time."

"I've never seen it," Bradley said.

"You just don't remember," she replied.

Bradley studied her for a moment; the fabric hugged her curves and emphasized every feminine attribute. "No, I would have remembered," he stated.

Mary blushed. "Well, I'm wearing it today, so get over it. Both of you."

A few minutes later Sean and Bradley were in the room next door and Mary was waiting for Kevin's arrival. As Bradley had predicted, a knock sounded on the suite's door at ten-thirty. Mary answered it.

"Wow, you look good," Kevin said, inviting himself into the suite. "I thought I'd come by a little early just to see how you were doing."

Mary smiled. "Thanks, that was nice of you. I'm doing okay. Sean said he'd let me know if anything changes with Bradley."

Kevin took her hand and brought it to his lips. "The idea for this outing is to make you forget about Bradley," he said. "So, first rule."

He kissed the tip of her finger.

"We don't mention his name. Second rule."

He kissed the next finger.

"You only think about me. Third rule."

He kissed another finger.

"I only think about you. And fourth rule."

He took her baby finger into his mouth and lightly sucked on it.

"We get much better acquainted with each other."

Mary slipped her hand from his grasp. *Really, did that work with other women?* she thought. *I wonder if he would be offended if I used some hand sanitizer?*

"Okay, this guy is just plain gross," Bradley whispered to Sean. "She's going have to disinfect that hand."

"Well, I'll just get my coat," Mary suggested, walking to the couch to pick it up.

Kevin grasped her arms and pulled her back against him. He lowered his mouth to her neck and kissed her. Mary was glad she was wearing a turtleneck.

"We could order in," he suggested. "I'm sure I could make our stay in your room pleasurable beyond your wildest imagination."

No self-esteem problem here, Mary thought.

"Wildest imagination? I'll show him wildest imagination," Bradley muttered.

Mary twisted her way out of his grasp. "As delightful as that sounds, I promised Sean that I would get out and get a change of scenery. And you know how demanding Sean can be."

"He's nothing but a tight ass, Mary," Kevin said, grabbing hold of her arms. "You don't have to listen to him."

"I'm a tight ass?" Sean whispered. "I'm a tight ass?"

Bradley nodded. "Yeah, you are, but it's always for a good reason."

Sean glared at Bradley.

"But Kevin, I always listen to my brother."

Both Sean and Bradley snorted.

Kevin pulled her closer. "He doesn't have to know, Mary," Kevin said. "It can be our little secret."

"That's it, I'm going in," Bradley growled.

Sean put a hand on Bradley's good shoulder to hold him down. "Give her a minute."

Mary put both hands on Kevin's chest and pushed him away. "Kevin, if I had wanted to be mauled, I would have gone to the zoo. I'm not in the mood, okay?"

Bradley and Sean grinned at each other.

Kevin shrugged. "All you had to say was no," he said.

Mary picked up her coat. "Okay, no, Kevin," she said. "So, do you still want to go to lunch?"

"Yeah, what the heck," he said, with a shrug. "Maybe I can charm you with my scintillating conversation."

Mary nodded. "You can try."

Chapter Twenty-six

The place was exactly as Sean had described; a small store-front restaurant with a scattering of tables covered with cheap plastic table cloths. Each table had plastic flowers in a vase in the middle and an assortment of hot sauces in a small plastic container.

The food smelled heavenly, and if Mary hadn't had knots in her stomach, she might have actually enjoyed it. Kevin greeted the owners by name and ushered Mary into a table near the corner. He sat so his back was against the wall and he was facing the door. *Typical cop seating,* Mary thought.

Mary glanced behind Kevin to Maria, the ghost who had been following him and tried to make eye contact, but the girl refused to look at her.

"What would you like to eat?" Kevin asked.

"I have to admit my stomach's been a little nervous lately," she said. "What do you suggest that's not too spicy?"

Kevin reached across the table and caught Mary's hand in his. "Babe, you need to relax," he said. "I could tell in the hotel room that something was bothering you."

Yeah, you, Mary thought. She looked up to respond and noticed Maria was staring at their clasped hands, her face filled with anger. Mary turned her hand over and intertwined her fingers with his. "You always did understand me," she said. "Perhaps better than I understand myself."

He smiled and brought their hands to his mouth. He kissed her hand and then turned it and pressed a kiss on her wrist. "I can feel your pulse racing," he said. "I know I excite you. I'd love to be able to show you just what you do to me."

Mary smiled at him while her stomach turned. "That could be nice," she said.

She quickly looked up and saw Maria staring at her. Hate filling her eyes. Their eyes met and Maria reacted with surprise. "You can see me?" she asked.

Mary smiled and nodded slightly.

"Mary, where did you go, sweetheart?" Kevin asked.

Mary turned back to Kevin. "I'm just taking all of this in," she lied. "I have a feeling this little restaurant is going to be fondly remembered."

His smile reminded her of a snake, cold and calculating. "Let's get take-out," he suggested. "My place isn't too far from here."

Mary considered the request for a moment, thought about how much evidence she would be able to find at his place. Then she considered how Sean and Bradley would react to that idea. No, that wasn't going to work. However, she didn't need to let Kevin know.

"Why don't you order for us while I go to the Ladies Room and freshen up before we leave," she said, trying to ease her hand out of his grip.

"Babe, you can freshen up at my place," he said, tightening his grip.

Mary smiled slowly, running her tongue over her lips. "Kevin, there might not be enough time."

He released her hand. "Hurry back," he choked.

Mary looked at Maria and subtly motioned to her to follow. The Ladies Room was in the back of the restaurant, next to the back door and loading area. Piles of black garbage bags and stacks of boxes filled the tiny hallway next to the bathroom. She opened the door and then made sure it was locked behind her. The floor was concrete, the fixtures were stained with rust and a half-used roll of paper towels sat on a shelf next to the toilet. Maria glided through the closed door.

"He's mine, you pig," Maria spat. "You leave him alone."

Mary nodded. "Okay, I'll leave him alone if you answer some questions."

"Really? You would give him up so easily?" she asked. "Why?"

Mary shrugged. "He's the kind of man who flits from woman to woman," she said. "I don't like to be a notch on some man's belt."

Maria sighed. "You're right, he is like that. But I love him."

"Sergeant Monroe told me about you," Mary said. "You're Maria Hernandez?"

Maria nodded. "Sergeant Monroe is a good man. How is he?"

"He's dead, Maria," she said. "He died the day you were supposed to go home."

Maria was surprised. "Go home? How could I go home?"

"Sergeant Monroe bought you a plane ticket," she said. "He had contacted your parents and they wanted you back."

Tears flowed down her translucent face. "Why didn't I go home?" she asked.

"Maria, how did you die?" Mary asked. "Do you remember?"

"I think it had something to do with this," she said and lifted her shirt.

Mary gasped. Maria's abdomen had been sliced open, two flaps of skin hung to the sides, exposing her internal organs.

"Who did this to you?" Mary asked.

"I can't remember," she sobbed. "The last thing I remember is Officer Brady telling me that he would take care of me when I was feeling sick. He loved me."

"He told you he loved you?"

Maria nodded. "He was so sweet, so tender. Not like the other men."

"Officer Brady had sex with you?"

"We made love together," she insisted. "He told me he loved me. It was different than the other men."

"Where did you meet Officer Brady?" Mary asked.

"By Navy Pier," she said. "That's where I hung out. Traffic is good there."

"Traffic?" Mary asked.

"You know, tourists looking for a good time," she said. "I could make some real money there."

"Did you have a pimp?"

"Yeah, sure," she said. "I met him at the bus station. I didn't, you know, didn't want to do this. I knew my parents wouldn't want me to... But he gave me some pills and then I didn't care anymore. I really needed the pills."

"What was your pimp's name?"

"Angelo. He said he was my angel and he would save me," she said. "But he didn't save me or any of the other girls."

"Did Officer Brady know Angelo?"

Maria nodded. "Yeah, they had an agreement," she said. "Officer Brady got to use the girls whenever he wanted and then he would look the other way when it came to the stuff Angelo was doing."

Mary knew that her time was running out. "Maria, do you know where your body is?" she asked. "Where are you buried?"

"Cold water," she said, "I remember cold water."

The pounding on the door startled them both. "Mary, is everything fine in there?" Kevin demanded.

"Yes, I'm fine," she said. "I'll be out in a minute."

She turned to Maria. "I'll find you," she whispered.

Maria nodded and faded away.

Mary turned on the faucet and let it run while she texted Sean. She washed her hands, dried them on the paper towels and opened the bathroom door. She nearly ran into Kevin. "Who were you talking to?" he asked, blocking her way back to the restaurant.

Mary stepped to the side and pushed open the door. "Really, Kevin? Does it look like I was having a party in there?"

Kevin looked around the bathroom. "I heard your voice."

"Of course you did," she said. "I left a message for Sean that I wouldn't be available for the rest of the afternoon." She ran a finger down his chest. "Wasn't that the plan?"

He pulled her to him and kissed her roughly. "Yeah, but I don't think I'm going to be done with you until tomorrow at the earliest."

It took all of her self-control to not wipe her arm across her mouth and get rid of his taste. "Well, it sounds like I'm in for an exciting time," she said, gently pulling out of his embrace. "Shall we leave?"

She started to move toward the safety of the restaurant, but was once again blocked. "We can leave through the back door," he said, running his hands over her hips and pulling her to him. "It's faster that way."

Her cell phone rang. "Don't answer it," Kevin said, trying to pull it away from her.

"I have to," she shrugged, "Sean will worry."

He slapped it out of her hands and it crashed to the floor, sliding across the floor. "You left him a message," he said. "He can deal with it."

"Excuse me," Mary said, pushing back against his chest. "You don't treat me like that."

"Baby, right now, you're in my territory," he said. "And I'm going to treat you anyway I like."

Mary looked at the man she had just been sitting with. His eyes were dilated and his nose was red. Cocaine.

"Did you just snort?" she asked.

He smiled. "Yeah. But don't worry, I've got some for you," he said, sliding his hands over her butt. "Makes the sex so much better."

She slid her hands onto his shoulders and smiled. Leaning back, she braced her foot against the wall. "It seems that we have a little miscommunication," she said. "Perhaps this will help."

She pushed her foot off the wall and brought her knee up between his legs with as much force as she could. Kevin dropped to the floor with a scream. Mary stooped down, scooped up her phone and turned back to Kevin. "No one treats me like that."

She stepped over him and walked to the front of the restaurant. Her hands were shaking. She knew that Kevin would have raped her if he had been given the chance. Sean rushed through the front door. "You can arrest him for assault and attempted rape," she said to his anxious face, her voice shaking. "And check him for drugs while you're at it. He's lying on the floor in the back."

He put his arms on her shoulders and looked at her. "You okay?"

She bit her lip and nodded. "It got a little scary there for a while," she admitted.

"My car's parked half a block away," he said. "Why don't you wait there?"

"Thanks."

She stumbled out the door and onto the sidewalk. Walking down the street, she found her legs were too wobbly to stand. She stumbled to a light pole and laid her head against it. A moment later she was encased by a pair of familiar arms. "Your shoulder," she protested.

"Shut up," he growled, holding her close and helping her down the street.

She buried her head in his chest and let the security of his arms replace the fear.

"I'm going to kill him," Bradley said. "If I ever get my hands on him…"

Mary shook her head. "It's not nice to hurt handicapped people," she murmured.

He stopped and looked down at her. "Handicapped?"

"I don't think he'll ever walk totally upright again," she replied, meeting his eyes.

He chuckled and pulled her close again. "That's my girl," he whispered into her hair.

Chapter Twenty-seven

"After you give your statement, I want you and Bradley out of town," Sean said. "No argument."

Mary sat forward in the regulation-issued chairs in Sean's office and got ready to fight. "No Sean," she said. "I'm not running away from this. I told Maria I would find her body and I'm not going to just let that drop."

"Listen, the guy probably carved her up and dropped her in the middle of the lake for all we know," he argued. "We may never find her."

"Well, you sure as hell won't find her without me," she said. "You can't see dead people."

"All you've got on Kevin is assault and attempted rape," Bradley said. "And he could argue that he misinterpreted her actions. He already has a number of witnesses in that restaurant who said that he and Mary were looking cozy."

"We got him on drugs," Sean added.

"Yeah, using might get him stripped from the force, but it's not going to put him away for very long," Mary said. "We need to get him on murder, and we don't have enough yet."

Sean stood up quickly, knocking his chair to the floor. "Dammit, don't you get it," he said. "I don't want your help. I don't want you to investigate.

I want you to go the hell home!" He turned away from her. "Mary, I don't want you to die again."

She stood, walked up behind him, wrapped her arms around his waist and laid her head on his back. "I love you, big brother," she said, "and I don't plan on dying. Besides, Kevin is in custody, all I'll be doing is following up with Maria."

"Face it, Sean," Bradley added. "She's right, your investigation is weak without the information she can get you. And I, for one, don't want this guy back on the streets."

Sean sighed. "Damn," he said his voice softer. "Why don't I ever get to win arguments with you?"

Mary chuckled. "Simple, because I'm always right."

Bradley snorted.

Sean turned around and hugged Mary, then held her away from him. "No danger," he said, "just interrogation. You just talk to the ghosts. Any real people show up, you pull out."

"Deal," she said.

Sean looked over her head to Bradley. "You're lead on this," he said. "If she gives you a hard time, fling her over your good shoulder and carry her back to Freeport."

Bradley grinned. "You've got a deal."

"Hey, wait," Mary began.

"Mary...shut up," Bradley and Sean said simultaneously, and they all laughed.

It was nearly midnight when they arrived at Navy Pier. They pulled into the parking lot and walked over to the front entrance. The ground was covered with several inches of snow, but a narrow path had been shoveled out. The wind whipped across the pier from the lake. Mary pulled her coat tighter and Bradley placed his arm around her.

"How are you doing?" she asked. "Is the cold going to bother you?"

"This is nothing," he said, "unless we decide we need to take a swim, I'll be fine."

Mary looked over to her right. She could hear the lake lapping up against the side of the pier, but the water and the night sky melded into inky darkness.

They moved into the main portion of the park. Bright holiday lights encircled tree limbs and light poles, reflecting off the snow in a twinkling winter wonderland. It was like an island of light in the midst of the gloom. They walked toward the amusement park that featured the one-hundred-fifty-foot high Ferris wheel.

Moving past the park, they walked alongside the empty exhibit buildings. The lights from the park cast eerie shadows on the snow. The tops of the pilings barely peeked through the drifts of snow piled to the side. "Careful here," Mary said. "If we slip on the ice, we could end up getting wet."

Mary saw Maria standing near the exhibit buildings. She was wearing a mini-skirt, a t-shirt and sandals. *She must be freezing*, was her first thought. *No, she must have died when it was still warm outside*, was her second thought.

Maria moved forward. "You came back," she said.

"I told you I'd help you," Mary said.

The ghost looked beyond Mary. "Who's that?"

"Hi, I'm Bradley," he said. "What's your name?"

"Maria," she said, smiling at him, "Maria Hernandez. You looking for a good time?"

"Maria, how old are you?" Mary asked.

Maria scowled at Mary. "Twenty-one," she said.

"The truth," Mary replied, "the real truth."

Maria pouted. "I'll be sixteen in August."

"Maria, what day is it today?" Bradley asked.

"Hey, I'm not your personal calendar," she said.

He smiled and nodded. "Yeah, I just wanted to know how many days until your birthday," he said.

She smiled. "Oh, okay, that's better," she purred, moving next to Bradley. "It's three weeks until my birthday. Do you want me to save that day for you?"

"Maria, we need to talk with you," Mary interrupted.

Maria ignored Mary. "We could go out to eat and maybe go dancing," she said, "then we could go to your place and party."

"Maria, you need to listen to Mary," he said. "She's helps people like you. She's really good at it."

Maria tossed her head. "What? Is she a nun or something?"

"No," Bradley shook his head. "She helps people who are lost find their way home."

"I ain't lost," she said. "I know where I am."

She looked around. "I'm..." She paused. "I was just on my way..."

She looked up at Mary and Bradley with tears in her eyes. "What happened to me?" she cried.

"That's what we want to find out," Mary said softly. "Do you remember talking with me at the restaurant today?"

Maria paused. "You were there with Officer Brady," she said. "You told me I could have him. But they took him away."

"You told me that you were buried in the water," Mary said. "I promised you I would help find your body."

Maria stared out into the night sky for a moment. "He told me he loved me," she sobbed. "He told me he was going to fix everything. He loved me."

"Can you remember anything from the last time you saw him?" Mary asked.

"We were supposed to party," she said. "He told me he had some really good stuff and he was going to share."

"Then what happened?" Bradley asked. "Try to remember."

"We went to his place," she said. She lowered her head in concentration.

"He gave me something to drink," she said. "Then we had sex. He was mean to me, he hurt me."

Tears flowed down her young face. Bradley's hands balled into fists, remembering Mary's statement about what Kevin tried to do to her. He could only imagine what Kevin would have done to the defenseless teenager.

"Okay, sweetheart," he said, softly. "Can you tell us any more?"

"He gave me some stuff," she said. "He told me it would really give me a trip. It was too wild. I didn't like it. I lost all control."

She stopped for a moment and gagged. "He stuffed things down my mouth," she said. "I kept wanting to gag, but I couldn't. He had his hands down my throat pushing the stuff into me. I couldn't breathe. I was crying."

"What did it look like?" Mary asked.

"It was bags, like plastic bags," she said. "He stuffed a lot of them down my throat."

Bradley felt sick. "Then what did he do?" he asked.

She looked up at them in shock. "He put me in the water," she said slowly. "It was so cold. I couldn't feel anything. I can't remember after that…"

"He killed you," Bradley said.

She shook her head and cried, "But I don't want to be dead. I want to go back home."

Mary felt the tears behind her eyes. "I'm so sorry, Maria," she said, her voice tight. "I can only help you move on."

"Move on?"

"Yes, go to heaven," Mary explained.

"God don't want no one like me," she said. "I'm one of those bad girls. That's probably why he let me get killed."

"God wants you," Mary said. "He wouldn't have sent me to help you if He hadn't."

Maria sniffled and turned to Bradley. "Is that true?"

Bradley nodded. "Yeah, she gets her orders from God," he said. "And He sent her out tonight, just to find you."

Maria smiled. "Yeah? Really?"

Mary nodded. "Yeah."

"Are you gonna help the other girls?" Maria asked.

"Other girls?" Bradley asked.

Maria pointed to the end of the pier. Mary walked away from Bradley until she could see the individual forms take shape. At least a dozen women walked toward her, all different ages and colors, but Mary could tell each had definitely been a prostitute.

"She can help us," Maria called to the others.

Mary turned to Bradley. "He killed them all," she said. "No wonder…"

"He wanted me dead," Bradley finished.

Chapter Twenty-eight

The Special Victims Unit offices were teeming with dead prostitutes waiting their turn to make a statement to Mary or Bradley. Because it was three in the morning, the rest of the office was empty.

"This place feels creepy," Sean said. "Like someone is watching you."

Mary looked at the blonde woman who'd been following Sean around the office, trying to get his attention. "Well, someone is," she said, "you just can't see her."

Sean shivered. "Thanks, Mary."

He went to his office and shut the door. The woman glided through the door after him. A minute later he came out. "How long is this going to take?" he asked.

Mary smiled. "Well, since we've decided to take these reports long-hand and not put them into the system, it's taking longer than usual."

"Yeah, well if you can tell me how to explain the reports to my superiors, you can use the computers," he replied.

"Good point," she answered. "We'll be as quick as we can."

In order for both of them to interact with the dead prostitutes, Mary and Bradley sat across from each other at a narrow table, their left hands clasped together, their right hands holding pens and filling out forms. They were able to take the information about each of the women they met at the pier. Each woman told a similar story and each story ended the same way – they remembered being placed in cold water.

Once the statement was given, each ghost would fade away. Mary was pretty sure they were heading back to the pier, the place they had spent the last days of their lives. She hoped if the police couldn't locate their physical remains, the capture of their killer would be enough to allow them to move on.

After the last form was filled out, Bradley sat back in the stiff wooden chair, stretched and yawned. He turned bleary eyes to Mary. "How are you doing?" he asked.

She yawned back and smiled. "I could use a nap," she said.

"Yeah, for a month," he agreed, "but food would be good too."

She nodded. "Eggs, bacon…"

Bradley smiled. "Waffles, pancakes…"

They looked at each other, grinned and said, "Diet soda."

Sean peeked his head out of his office. "Are they gone?"

"Yeah, except for the one who wants to haunt you for life," Mary said.

Sean turned quickly. "What?"

"Just kidding."

Sean sat down at the table with them and picked up all of the reports. "So, what do we have here?"

"Mules," Bradley said. "These women were forced fed drugs and then, later on, the drugs were removed."

"Surgically removed," Mary added. "They were all sliced open."

Sean shook his head. "This doesn't make sense," he said. "These women were in Chicago, not Mexico, why would they need mules here?"

"Another odd fact," Bradley said. "I don't think they were dead when the drugs were removed."

"Why would you say that?" Mary asked.

Bradley sat back in his chair. "The ghosts we've seen today resemble what they looked like when death occurred, right?"

Mary nodded. "Yeah, we see them in the condition they are in when their spirit leaves their body."

"So, why are we seeing sliced stomachs if that happened after death?"

"But they remembered dying," Sean said.

"Or they thought they were dying," Bradley said. "They remember being put in cold water. Hypothermia can produce a slowing of your system and induce a coma-like state. I'm a recent expert on that."

"So they lowered their core temperatures in the water?" Mary asked.

198

Bradley nodded. "You get it down to about sixty-five degrees and you have a body that looks dead. No pupil response, waxy skin, no discernible heartbeat."

"But we're still back at why," Sean said. "Why go through all the trouble to turn them into cadaver mules?"

"Where can cadavers go where live people can't?" Mary asked.

"Medical schools," Bradley said. "Colleges, universities…places where pushers might have a hard time getting into."

"So, you have a contact at a med school. You send bodies into a temperature-controlled location," Sean said. "Then your contact dissects the stomach, removes the drugs and leaves the rest of the body available for further use at the school."

"And when they're done, they cremate the remains," Mary added. "Evidence destroyed."

"Damn…brilliant," Sean said. "I wonder how long he's been doing this."

"Well, he won't be doing it any longer," Bradley said. "There's got to be some of those bodies still out at the schools. Once we locate a couple of them and get some of the contacts to turn state's evidence, he'll be in a temperature-controlled climate of his very own for a long time."

"You've both done a great job," Sean said. "There is no way we would have tracked this down so quickly. Thank you."

Mary nodded. "Thanks. But it's kind of bittersweet," she said. "What the hell happened to Kevin?"

"We may never find out," Sean said, standing up and slipping the reports into a folder. "Now, not to sound like an ungrateful host…but get the hell out of my city."

Bradley laughed. "Yeah, not to sound like an ungrateful guest, but the further away I get from Chicago, the better."

Chapter Twenty-nine

The sun was shining brightly and reflecting off the snow covered farmland surrounding Freeport. Bradley had the radio on and holiday music filled the interior of the car.

"I know I should be tired," Mary said, "but I feel so pumped."

Bradley laughed. "I know exactly how you feel," he said, taking a deep breath. "Like the world's a little better place and you got to help."

She smiled at him. "Yes, exactly! And hopefully things can get back to normal again."

Bradley turned down the street to Mary's house. It felt like she hadn't been home for a month, not just a week. She was delighted to see Andy Brennan busily shoveling her walk. *Yeah, normal was good.*

They pulled up to the curb and got out of the car.

"Hey, Miss O'Reilly, where've you've been? You get arrested or something?" Andy called.

"Why does everyone always think the worst of me?" she asked Bradley with a grin.

She scooped up a handful of snow, packed it lightly, turned and then threw it at Andy. "Yeah, I got arrested for assault with a snowball."

The snowball landed with a splat on Andy's chest. He looked down, amazed. "You have really good aim," he said, scooping up some snow of his own. "But can you dodge?"

He whipped the snowball toward her, hurtling it with surprising force. At the last moment, she pulled Bradley in front of her as a shield. Surprised, Bradley didn't have time to react and the snowball barreled into his face and down his neck.

Mary peeked around Bradley and looked up at his snow covered face. "Wow, looks like I'm not the only one spending some time in jail," she said.

Bradley glared at Mary.

"All right young man," Bradley growled, "I want you to turn around and place your hands on your head, where I can see them."

Andy immediately did as he was told, a flicker of apprehension in his eyes.

Bradley moved forward, toward the young man. "Do you know what the penalty is for assaulting an officer?" he asked.

Andy shook his head. "No, sir."

"Do you think it's funny to throw snowballs at officers of the law?" he asked.

"No, sir. I wasn't trying to hit you. But Miss O'Reilly moved."

Bradley moved closer. "That's true," he said. "Do you feel that Miss O'Reilly deserves to be assaulted with a snowball?"

"Do you want the truth, sir?"

A grin stole over Bradley's face; he squatted down next to Andy. "Yes, young man, the truth."

Mary watched Bradley walk over to the boy and squat down next to him. His broad back blocked her view of Andy. She was sure Bradley would take the incident in the spirit of fun.

Bradley seemed to be listening to something Andy was saying and nodding. Mary peered closer. They looked like they were exchanging a handshake or something. "Is everything okay over there?" she called.

"Fine," Bradley answered, "we're just figuring some things out. Man stuff."

"Yeah, man stuff," Andy replied.

"Oh, okay," Mary answered. "Could I be of assistance at all?"

"No, you just stay right where you are," Bradley answered.

Andy giggled.

Oh, crap, Mary thought. *This is not going to end well...*

Before she could complete her thought, the air was filled with a barrage of snowballs all directed at her. The first two connected and hit her in the head. The next two exploded on her back as she ran for cover. The rest flew over her head, as she sat in the snow behind a drift, creating ammunition.

She sat quietly, the seat of her pants getting cold and wet. *It's worth it,* she silently reminded herself.

In a few moments she heard what she'd been waiting for. "Mary? Mary? Are you okay?" Bradley's voice called.

She smiled wickedly, loaded a snowball into each hand and waited.

"Miss O'Reilly," Andy called. "Maybe she got hurt."

Mary almost felt bad about making them worry. She glanced over at the pile of snowballs waiting for her retaliation. *Almost, but not really*, she mused.

"Mary, this isn't funny," Bradley called. "Just let us know you're okay."

She could tell he was getting closer. She bit her lip and listened to the crunching of footsteps in the snow.

Any moment now.

The footsteps stopped on the other side of the drift. "Mary," Bradley called once again.

She sighed. *Maybe I should let them know...*

A shadow caught her eye. She looked up to find an avalanche of snow descending on her. Her head, face and shoulders were suddenly covered with snow.

"Yes!" Andy shouted and slapped Bradley's hand. "We took her down!"

Bradley peered over the drift. "Um, Mary," he said, scratching the side of his head innocently, "seems like you got a little snow on your head."

Mary hefted two snowballs. "I'll show you a little snow," she yelled as she whipped Bradley and Andy with the remainder of her cache.

Five minutes later, three out of breath and snow-laden warriors pulled the luggage from Bradley's car and carried it into Mary's house. She looked at the boy and the man, covered with snow, faces red from the cold and still grinning from ear to ear. "Take your coats off and hang them in the bathroom," she ordered. "I'll make hot chocolate."

"Cool!" Andy cried, racing to the bathroom.

"Yeah, cool," Bradley said, following Mary into the kitchen.

She turned and found him standing behind her. She raised an eyebrow. "You're melting on my kitchen floor."

He grinned. "Yeah, you too."

She looked down and saw that she was indeed dropping bits and pieces of snow from her outerwear. She looked up and found him staring at her. "What?" she asked, her voice a little shaky.

He lifted his hand and wiped away some snow still clinging to her hair. "You throw a mean snowball, Mary O'Reilly," he said softly. "Welcome home."

Chapter Thirty

Mary muted the holiday music as she reached over to answer the ringing phone. "Mary O'Reilly."

"Hey, Mary, it's Sean."

Her brother's voice had a bit of an edge to it. "How are you doing?"

"Good, no, actually great," she replied. "I spent the rest of Saturday cleaning my house and I was a total lazy bum on Sunday. I watched 'It's A Wonderful Life' and 'A Muppet's Christmas Carol' and ate junk food. So, what's up?"

"Is Bradley around?" he asked.

"Sean, he works three blocks away from me," she said. "Why would he be around?"

The bell over her door sounded and Mary turned around to see Bradley enter the office.

"How did you do that?" she asked Sean.

Bradley slipped his coat off and hung it on the coat rack. She could tell he was still favoring his injured shoulder. "Sean called me and told me to head over here," Bradley explained, sitting in the chair on the other side of her desk. "He said he wanted to share some information with both of us."

"Okay, Sean, I'm going to put you on speaker phone," she said, pressing the button and placing the handset back into the cradle. "Can you hear us?"

"Yeah, we're good," Sean replied. "I wanted to catch you up on the developments of Kevin's case. The reports you guys pulled together have been very helpful. We've been able to track down about half the bodies at medical schools throughout the state. Maria Hernandez was one of the first bodies found. We've contacted her parents."

"That's great, Sean," Bradley interrupted. "But cut to the chase. You wouldn't have asked us to be here together just to give us that kind of an update."

Sean paused. "Kevin's out," he said.

"What?" Mary replied, sitting back in her seat.

"We only had him for assault; we didn't have enough for the murder charges," he said. "He paid his bail and walked."

"When?" Bradley asked.

"Yesterday," Sean said. "I didn't find out about it until this morning."

"Damn," Bradley replied.

"What else?" Mary asked.

"Angelo was found dead this morning," Sean said. "Overdose. At least that's what it was supposed to look like."

"How long has he been dead?" Bradley asked.

"A couple of hours at the most," Sean replied. "I want you two back here in Chicago, protective custody."

"No way," Mary said. "Sean I can't go into hiding because Kevin's loose. We don't even know if he'll come here."

Bradley nodded. "I agree with Mary," he said. "We're actually safer here. We know the territory, we know the people. Why would he come after us? Unless there's something else you're not telling us."

"I found out Kevin was free because there was a note on my desk this morning from him," he said. "It said he was sorry it had to end this way. He'd always considered me a friend. But he was going to make Mary pay for setting him up."

"Nothing about me?" Bradley said. "I'm disappointed."

"Well, yeah, you were mentioned," Sean said. "And it's not very complimentary either."

"So, we know he's coming," Mary said. "He doesn't have the element of surprise. He doesn't know Freeport and he's not a familiar face. I still believe we are safer staying here."

"Damn it, I've got to run this case in Chicago. I can't come out and protect you," Sean said.

"Um, when did you become my big brother too?" Bradley asked. "Sean, we are both trained professionals. We know what we're doing. We won't take any chances. You keep doing what you're doing and we'll keep in touch."

Bradley reached over and hung up the phone. Mary smiled. "He's going to be really mad," she said.

"He'll get over it. Now, what are we going to do?"

Mary rubbed her hands over her arms. "I'm not going to hide somewhere until he's found," she said. "If he's looking for me, the sooner he tries something, the sooner we catch him."

Bradley nodded. "Okay, we won't hide," he said. "But I think it's imperative we take protective measures."

"I agree."

Bradley looked at the large glass windows on the front of Mary's office. "You're a sitting duck here," he said. "And if you close the blinds, you can't see what's coming."

"I don't think he's going to just shoot me through a window," she said. "He wants to take care of me up close and personal."

He stood up, walked away from the desk and ran his hand through his hair. "Yeah, I know. Mary..."

"Don't even say it," she interrupted. "I'll take precautions, but I'm not going into protective custody."

"What's your idea of precautions?" he asked.

"I can work from home for a week or so. I have wireless access there and I can switch my phone so it goes to the house," she said. "If I have to go into the office, I'll do it during the day when people are around."

"Okay, that's reasonable."

"I'll take someone with me if I go shopping or take any local trips," she added. "I won't be alone in a place I can get snatched."

"That sounds good too."

She looked at him, standing in the corner of her office, his arms crossed over his chest and his stance determined. She sighed. "And I suppose you will be sleeping in my guest room for the next little while."

He nodded. "Oh, without a doubt."

"Bradley, I really don't need a babysitter," she argued.

"Who said anything about you?" he asked, walking over to the rack and grabbing his coat. "I'm expecting you to protect me."

She couldn't help it…she grinned.

"I'll be back here in an hour," he said, "to help you carry whatever you need from the office to your house. In the meantime, I'm calling a patrol car to hang out in front of your shop, so you can close your blinds."

Mary stood and followed him to the door. "Just remember you aren't his favorite person either," she said. "You need to take precautions, too."

He nodded. "So much for normal."

"Yeah, it was fun while it lasted."

Chapter Thirty-one

"Is it safe?" Stanley called from the doorway.

Mary jumped and then caught her breath. "Of course it's safe," she said. "What did you expect?"

Stanley shrugged. "Well, you have your blinds drawn in the middle of the day and I saw our favorite police chief head this way," he explained. "I figured you and he were finally...well, you know...and you needed a little privacy."

"So, you came over?" she asked.

"I yelled before I came in," he said. "Besides that busy-body Rosie is headed down the street, so I wanted to give you two a chance to get decent."

Mary laughed. "Yeah, Rosie is the busy-body."

The bell over the door announced Rosie's arrival. "I'm a busy-body?" she asked. "Well, of course I am. But really, you don't need to advertise it."

Mary laughed. "Stanley and I were discussing the actuality of which one of you is more nosey."

"Well, when I saw your blinds drawn in the middle of the day, I just had to see what was going on," Rosie admitted. She glanced around the room. "Chief Alden isn't hiding in the closet, is he, dear?"

"No, he's not," she said. "And we are not planning on having sex in the middle of my office in the middle of the day."

"So when are you planning on having sex?" Stanley asked.

The bell over the door rang once again. "Who's planning on having sex?" Bradley asked.

Mary laid her head in her hands and shook her head. "I'm living in a sitcom."

"You think having a murderer gunning for you is funny?" Bradley asked. "You really have a weird sense of humor."

"A murderer?" Rosie gasped.

"Gunning for our Mary?" Stanley added. "Well, what the hell are you going to do about it, Chief?"

"Stanley, Bradley is here to help me move things to my house, so I can work from there for a while," she explained. "And I've assured him that I won't go anywhere without a friend. So I'll probably be bugging the two of you when I need to go somewhere."

"Oh, Mary, that's no problem at all," Rosie said. She turned to Bradley. "Should I be packing heat?"

"Rosie, as a sworn law enforcement officer in the state of Illinois, I have to inform you that it is illegal to carry a concealed firearm on your person," Bradley said.

Stanley snorted. "What he's saying is, yes, you ninny, pack heat, but don't tell him about it."

212

"That's not exactly what I was saying," Bradley began.

"Don't worry about it, Chief," Stanley interrupted. "We know what to do. So how are you getting Mary out of here?"

Bradley shrugged. "My cruiser is at the curb in front of the office."

"Ain't you got no imagination?" Stanley blustered. "If she's a sitting duck with her blinds open, don't you think both of you carrying her stuff out to your cruiser will be open season? I'll pull old Betsey around back and Mary can pile her stuff in there."

Rosie peered at the door. "Do you think he's on top of one of the buildings, waiting to shoot us?"

Bradley shook his head. "I don't think he's a sniper, Rosie," he said. "But we really shouldn't discount any possibility."

"Well, I think it's horrid that someone would try to kill you at Christmastime," she said.

"Yeah, after the holidays is much better," Stanley muttered. "Darn fool woman."

"I heard that Stanley," Rosie said.

"I'm going to get my car," Stanley said. "I'll be back in five minutes."

Stanley walked to the door, peered out and then left.

"Well, it looks like it's safe," Rosie said. "Mary, I'll go and pick up some groceries for you. What do you need?"

"Diet soda," Bradley and Mary said at the same time.

Rosie turned to Bradley. "Are you staying with Mary?"

Bradley nodded. "Yes, we thought it would be safer if I stayed at Mary's," he said, "in her guest room."

Rosie smiled. "That's wonderful! Wait until I tell Stanley! He'll be so excited. I knew you weren't gay."

Rosie hurried out the door, so excited about her news she didn't remember about the potential threat.

"What was that all about?" Bradley asked.

Mary smiled innocently. "They're just really happy you're protecting me."

Chapter Thirty-two

"So, what did you learn about Private Kenney?" Mary asked, as she dished beef stew out of a large pot on her stove.

"Well, his mother is the Kenney I was thinking of," Rosie said, tossing a salad at the counter. "And he went to Freeport High School, graduated with the class of 1964."

"His best friend was Bob Sterling," Stanley added, standing at the counter buttering a hot roll.

"Hey, I know Bob Sterling," Bradley said, sitting at the table. "He's on the Fire and Police Commission. He's a good guy."

"Yeah, those two were thick as thieves when they were young," Stanley said, chuckling and buttering another roll. "Can't remember the number of times I caught them in my crab apple tree."

"Did they serve together in Vietnam?" Mary asked.

Rosie nodded, carrying the salad to the table. "Yes, they did," she said. "Bob was with Pat when he died. They said it changed his life. He never married."

"Yeah, death is a life changing event," Mary said, "no matter which side of the fence you're standing on."

Mary carried the bowls to the table and snatched the basket of rolls from Stanley. "You know we were going to share these," she scolded.

"Well, if you're going to be selfish," Stanley grumbled, taking his place at the table.

"Thanks for saving them," Bradley said. "I was getting worried."

Rosie laughed. "I think there's plenty of food to go around."

"So, getting back to business," Mary teased. "Was there anyone else in town that was his friend?"

"You know, he was sweet on that gal over at the Courthouse…Linda Lincoln," Stanley said.

"Really?" Mary replied. "Linda? She is the sweetest person in the world."

"Yeah, she lost her husband back about a year ago," Rosie said. "Poor thing."

"Wow! I didn't know."

"Well, I think you'd just come into town," Rosie explained. "You probably hadn't even met her yet. Must be hard to lose two people you love."

"I can't imagine," Bradley said.

"Well, maybe you don't love the second one as much as the first," Stanley suggested. "Maybe you play it safe, so your heart won't get banged up."

"Seems to me that you can't pick when you fall in love," Rosie said. "You can only choose to accept it and enjoy it, or run away from it."

"Spoken like a gal who has enjoyed her fill of being in love," Stanley said.

"Nothing wrong with being in love," Rosie grinned. "It's my favorite pastime."

"Getting back to Private Kenney…I wonder if his personal effects were sent home," Mary said. "It seems the letter he's looking for is the key."

"Do you want me to approach his mother?" Rosie asked. "I can say the Historical Society is thinking about doing something to honor Veterans next year and wondered if she still had some of his things we could borrow."

"That would be wonderful, Rosie," Mary said. "Then we aren't opening up too many old wounds."

Rosie and Stanley left after dinner; Mary pulled her laptop out and sat in front of the fireplace. Bradley sat on the couch flipping through some reports. Suddenly Mary sat up straight. "What?" Bradley asked, instantly alert.

"I just realized…" Mary said, a little bit of panic in her voice.

Bradley sat down next to her on the floor. "What? What is it?"

"It's after the first of December and I still don't have my Christmas tree up."

Bradley exhaled deeply. "You're kidding, right?"

Mary shook her head. "No, my family usually puts the tree up the day after Thanksgiving. I've wasted a whole week."

"I don't think I would classify what we did last week as *wasting*," he said.

She smiled. "Yeah, but we don't have any excuses now."

"What? It's dark outside," he protested. "We can't find a tree in the dark."

"Oh, I already have my tree," she said. "I went to the tree farm and cut it the day before Thanksgiving, to beat the rush. It's in my garage in a bucket of water."

"And you want me to…"

"Please Bradley?"

He rubbed his shoulder. "I don't know, I have this wound," he began.

"I'll make popcorn," she said.

"Real popcorn? Not microwave?"

"Real popcorn with real butter."

Bradley sighed. "You run a hard bargain, Mary O'Reilly," he said with a smile. "Where's the tree stand?"

"In the box next to the tree," she said.

A few minutes later Bradley came back in carrying the tree. "This is it?" he asked. "This is your tree?"

Mary looked at the slightly lopsided and scrawny tree and nodded.

"I thought you went early," he said. "This was all they had left?"

"No," Mary admitted, feeling slightly embarrassed. "It's a Rudolph Tree."

"A what?"

"You know," she sang. "All of the other reindeer used to laugh and call him names; they never let poor Rudolph join in any reindeer games."

Bradley shook his head. "Sorry, still not getting it."

"Well, all of the other trees were big and bushy and symmetrical, and there was my tree, lopsided and a little bare and all by himself."

"Because all of the other Christmas trees wouldn't let him join in any Christmas tree games?" Bradley asked.

"Exactly!" Mary said with a smile.

"Mary," Bradley said patiently, "there are no such things as Christmas tree games."

"Ha! A couple months ago you thought there were no such things as ghosts," she countered.

He paused, looked at her and looked at the tree. "You're kidding, right?"

She giggled. "Yeah, but I did feel sorry for it," she said. "Do you think it will look really bad?"

"No, Mary, I think it will be the most beautiful tree because it's the best loved."

"Bradley, you're a poet."

"No, I'm just beginning to see the world from a different perspective."

Two hours later, the popcorn was popped and devoured, and Bradley was putting the angel on the top of the tree. Mary stood back, watching him, her hands clasped in excitement. "Oh, this is just beautiful, you did a great job," she said.

"Yeah, imagine my surprise when I found that all of your lights weren't neatly put away in last year's containers," he grumbled.

"But didn't that make you feel more at home?" she asked.

He turned and glared at her. "No!"

She laughed out loud. "Okay, a little more to the left and she will be perfect," Mary directed.

Bradley twisted the angel to the left and stood back.

"Now comes the best part," Mary said. "When I say three, you need to switch off the living room lights."

Bradley positioned himself next to the light switch and Mary knelt down next to the tree. She plugged the tree in and yelled, "Three!"

Bradley flipped the switch; now all of the lights in the house were off. The little tree illuminated the room in sparkles of white, green, red and blue. "Isn't this great?" she asked, moving next to him and looking at the tree.

He had to admit the transformation was amazing. *Who would have thought such a scrawny tree could end up being so beautiful? Mary would.*

He glanced down at her upturned face, joy written clearly across it. *Where's the mistletoe when you need it?* he thought.

Chapter Thirty-three

"Hi, Linda, this is Mary O'Reilly. How are you doing?"

Mary sat back on her couch and put her feet up. *Working from home wasn't too bad after all.*

"I'm working on a case and I heard you might be able to help me on it," she continued. "I was wondering if you'd like to come over for lunch today. I'm working from home and I have a spinach quiche in the oven."

Mary nodded.

"How does eleven-thirty sound? Perfect. See you then."

She put the phone down, walked over to look at her Christmas tree and smiled. In the light of day she could see the little imperfections the night-time Christmas lights hid. She grinned at the large clumps of tinsel Bradley had tossed at the tree. *No, Mary, this is more realistic*, he'd said.

"What's realistic about tinsel? It's not like it grows naturally," Mary said, shaking her head and separating the strands.

"Hey, are you fixing my tinsel?"

Mary jumped and then turned around. She took one look at Bradley and her heart flipped over in her chest. *Dang, he looks good in his uniform, all fresh shaven and smelling like a man.*

"I wasn't fixing it," she lied. "I was examining it so I can make mine more realistic in the future."

He laughed. "Remind me never to use you in court on my side."

"Why not?" she asked. "I always tell the truth."

Bradley snorted.

"Hey, there are muffins on the counter, if you're interested."

"Blueberry muffins?" he asked.

She grinned. "Are there any other kind?"

Bradley grabbed a muffin and bit into it. "So, if we never catch Kevin, can I live here forever?"

She laughed. "I don't know how your wife would feel..." She stopped and bit her lip. "Sorry, that was fairly thoughtless of me," she said.

"Don't worry about it," he said with a shrug. "I know it's a strange situation."

She nodded. "Yeah, I understand strange situations. I live one."

He laughed and grabbed a second muffin. "I'll be at the station most of the day," he said. "Are you going to be okay?"

"Linda's coming over for lunch. I want to ask her about Patrick Kenney," she said. "Then I'm thinking of going with Rosie to Patrick's mother's house."

"Okay, just be careful out there," he said with a smile.

"Yes, sir!"

Linda Lincoln's title was County Clerk, but anyone who had any dealings with her realized that she single-handedly ran the county. If she didn't personally have the information you needed in her steel-trap of a mind, she could put her fingers on it in moments. She was simply amazing and Mary really admired her.

She arrived precisely at eleven-thirty and offered Mary a small pot of narcissus wrapped in a plaid Christmas fabric and bright red bow. "They are so beautiful," Mary said. "Thank you."

"It's not every day I get such a nice invitation to lunch," Linda replied. "It's the least I can do. Besides, Deininger Floral Shop had them in the window and I couldn't resist. I bought another pot for myself."

"They must love you there," Mary laughed, setting the flowers in the middle of the table.

"Well, they do tend to wave me over when they have something new in their window," she said with a smile. "And I don't have a whole lot of willpower."

Mary offered Linda a seat and brought the lunch over. They ate and chatted about the city and the various people and shops in town. Finally, when they were done, Mary filled Linda's glass again and took out her notepad.

"Do you mind if I ask you a couple of questions?"

"No, I don't mind at all," Linda offered.

"This might be a little personal," Mary warned.

"Okay, now I'm intrigued," she said. "Whatever could you be working on that would involve me?"

"Private Patrick Kenney," Mary said.

Linda took a deep breath and sat back against her chair. "Patrick. It's been such a long time since someone said his name," she said.

"Does it hurt for you to talk about him?" Mary asked.

"No. That was a long time ago," she said, "a different lifetime ago."

"I understand you dated Patrick in high school and then when he was deployed; you were waiting for him?"

"Yes," Linda said, "we dated throughout high school and I said I'd wait for him. But at the time it was just what you said. You know, you don't really understand what you're agreeing to, but it sounds so dramatic and noble. High school girls are nothing, if not dramatic."

Mary laughed. "Oh, yes, I remember those days."

"But something happened to Patrick over there that changed him," she said. "Suddenly his letters were deeper, more thoughtful. They were poetry. I really fell in love with Patrick when he was overseas."

"Letters were important to both of you?" Mary asked.

Linda nodded. "Yes, in those days you lived for letters. There was no other way to communicate. And letters could take weeks to get back home," she explained. "I rushed to the mailbox every day in hopes of getting another letter from Patrick."

"Wow, it sounds like he was incredible."

"The boy that left Freeport was just that, a boy," she said. "But the man that wrote me those letters... He stole my heart and, in all honesty, I never got it back again."

Mary was surprised. "But you were married..."

"Charlie, my husband, was a good man," she said. "And I was good to him. But you only love like I did once. I loved Charlie as much as I was able and we were happy."

"When did you receive your last letter from Patrick?"

"About a month before...before he died," she said. "I had been expecting one when his mother received the news about his death. I was lost for the longest time. I wanted to die too, but I knew that he would want me to go on."

"And you met Charlie."

"Yes, I met Charlie and it seemed like the right thing to do," she said.

"Did you receive any of his personal effects?" Mary asked.

Linda shook her head. "No, we weren't officially engaged or anything, so his mother received those," she said. "Really, it was for the best."

"How about Bob Sterling?"

Linda smiled. "Good old Bob, he was Patrick's best friend. Actually, he looked me up once he got back home. It was great to see him again. But by that time I was married to Charlie, and I think we both felt a little uncomfortable talking about Patrick in front of him."

"Do you see him now?"

Linda shook her head. "No, you know, I haven't seen him for years. I really ought to try and get together with him. It would be nice to visit about old times."

"That's a nice idea," Mary said. "I'm sure Patrick would have liked that."

Chapter Thirty-four

"I'm packing," Rosie whispered to Mary as they left her house.

"You're what?" Mary asked.

Rosie patted her large purse. "I'm packing."

"Rosie, carrying a concealed weapon is not only illegal, it's dangerous. You could hurt someone."

"It's not a gun," Rosie replied. "It's wasp spray."

"What? Are you expecting some kind of insect attack?"

"No, silly, I'm surprised you don't know this, being a former police officer and all," she said. "I got an e-mail that said women should carry wasp spray in their purses because the stream travels a long distance and it could burn someone's eyes."

"Unless the wind is blowing in the wrong direction," Mary said, "and you end up with the spray in your eyes."

"Oh, I hadn't thought of that," Rosie admitted. "Well, hmmmm, I'm going to have to think of something else to protect you."

Mary gave Rosie a quick hug. "Thank you, Rosie, but I think you just being with me is protection enough."

Rosie pulled the large aerosol container from her purse. "Do you need any wasp spray, Mary?"

Mary looked around at the snow covered lawns and houses around her. "Well, not today," she laughed, "but perhaps in a couple of months."

They drove in Mary's car to Cherokee Hills, a subdivision on the west side of Freeport. Mary parked in front of a tidy tri-level decorated for the season with blinking lights and greenery. "What did you tell her?" Mary asked Rosie as they walked up to the front porch.

"That the Historical Society might be doing something about Veterans next year and I thought of her," Rosie said. "I was very non-committal."

"Thank you," Mary said. "I don't want her to worry her son isn't resting peacefully after all these years."

They rang the doorbell and waited for only a moment until a pleasant elderly woman with soft white hair, sparkling gray eyes and a welcoming smile answered the door. "Hello, come in," she said. "I'm Elaine Kenney, Patrick's mother." She paused and smiled sadly. "It's been quite a while since I introduced myself like that."

"I hope that our being here isn't going to cause you distress," Mary said.

Elaine shook her head and smiled at Mary. "Oh, no, it's about time all this got settled."

"I beg your pardon?" Mary asked.

"Patrick has been hanging around for much too long," she said. "It always gets worse during this

228

time of the year. I had heard about you, my dear. So, I told Patrick that instead of moaning about it, he needed to go over and see you. I see he did."

Mary was dumbfounded. "Yes, as a matter of fact, he did."

Elaine smiled. "So, what do you need?"

"I need to look through his personal effects and see if I can solve this mystery."

Elaine brought them into a sun-drenched living room filled with light-colored furniture with small floral prints. Mary and Rosie sat on the couch while Elaine opened an old chest. "This is all they sent me back," she said and placed a worn orange-crate sized shipping box on top of her coffee table.

Mary lifted the lid and placed it down next to the box. She moved aside the aged tissue paper that held the young soldier's final effects and carefully lifted out his dress uniform, military portrait and a box with his medals.

Underneath was an old cigar box. Mary lifted the box out, set it on the table and lifted the lid. Inside were two sets of letters, each wrapped together with a rubber band and two loose letters underneath them.

Mary looked through the first set. They were letters from home. There were letters from his mother, his father and Linda. Mary wondered if Linda would be happy to know he saved her letters.

The second set of letters was not in envelopes, they were plain white military stationary. Mary pulled one out and opened it. It was addressed to Linda.

"He must have saved copies of the letters he wrote to Linda," Mary said.

She handed the letter to Elaine. "Why that's strange," Elaine said.

"What's strange?" Rosie asked.

Elaine walked back to the chest and pulled out a square metal canister. Inside were letters, lovingly wrapped in tissue paper. Elaine pulled one out and handed it Mary. "He wrote his letters to us in different handwriting than he used when writing to Linda."

Mary looked at the two letters. They were definitely written by someone else.

She picked up the two loose letters. One letter was written in the same handwriting as the saved letters to Linda and the other, which matched the first letter word for word, was written in Patrick's handwriting.

"What do you think of this?" Mary asked, handing both letters to Elaine.

"Well, someone else was composing these love letters for Linda," Elaine said.

"How do you know?" Mary asked.

Elaine handed Mary the two second pages of the letter that Mary hadn't looked at. "Patrick hadn't finished copying the second page yet."

Chapter Thirty-five

"Mary, what are you doing up?" Bradley asked, wiping the sleep from his eyes. "It's three o'clock."

"I'm waiting for someone," she said simply, pulling the plush throw tighter around her legs. "He'll be here soon."

Bradley sat down next to her on the couch and yawned. "Are we waiting for Private Kenney?" he asked.

Mary nodded. "He has the most exceptional mother," Mary said. "I've never met anyone quite like her."

Bradley laid his head on the back of the couch. "I can guarantee that she's never met anyone like you either."

Mary turned and smiled at him. "Thanks! Would you be willing to help me with this one?"

Bradley yawned again. "Sure, what do you need?"

"Well, he's a military guy and you were a military guy, so I figured you might communicate better with each other. Does that make sense?"

"Mary, when did things making sense enter into anything we do?"

She lightly punched his arm.

"Ouch, you just damaged my wound."

She snorted. "You are such a baby."

The she heard the rustling in the kitchen. "Bradley, hold my hand."

"You're getting a little forward," he quipped, while enveloping her hand in his.

He immediately saw the young soldier going through the cabinets. "Private Kenney, I presume."

Mary nodded and they both got up and walked to the kitchen.

"Private Kenney," Mary said.

"Ma'am," Patrick responded. "Yes, ma'am."

"At ease soldier," Bradley said. "I apologize for being out of uniform, young man. I'm Master Sergeant Bradley Alden, 75th Regiment."

"A Ranger, sir?" Patrick saluted. "I'm honored."

"No, I'm the one who's honored," Bradley said. "How can we help you?"

Patrick looked around the kitchen in confusion. "I lost a letter…"

Mary placed the two letters she borrowed from Elaine on the counter. "Are these the letters you were looking for?"

Patrick scanned the letters and looked up at Mary with a smile. "Yes, ma'am, these are the letters," he said. "She needs to know. I wanted to tell her. I meant to tell her. But then…it was too late."

"Linda is my friend. I can tell her if you'd like."

He nodded. "You've got to tell her that I liked her and all," he shrugged. "But I didn't love her. Not

232

like I should. But Bob, he loved her and never told her because she was with me."

"Bob Sterling?" Bradley asked.

"Yes sir," Patrick smiled. "Sterling. He was so crazy about her that he'd write her these letters that he was never going to mail. I found them, tucked under his pillow. I thought they were really great letters, so I started copying them and mailing them to her."

"Did Bob find out?"

Patrick nodded. "He was pretty angry at first, but then he liked the idea that she would get to see his words and maybe, when he got back home we could both go and explain to her. But..."

"But you got shot and by the time Bob got home, Linda was already married."

"Yes, ma'am," he said. He looked at Bradley. "It's not too late, is it, sir? It's not too late to tell Linda the truth?"

"No, you're right; it's never too late for a chance at love, Private."

"You'll tell them? Won't you, ma'am? You'll let them know?"

"Yes, Patrick, I'll let them know."

He yawned. "I'm feeling pretty tired now, like I can finally rest."

"Yes, you've done what you needed to do," Mary said.

"I need to go say goodbye to my mom, she'll be waiting up," he said with a smile. "Then I'll finally get transferred. Thank you."

He saluted Mary and Bradley and faded away.

Mary wiped her eyes with her sleeve. Bradley caught her chin in his hand and looked down at her. "Hey, isn't this the happy part because he gets to move on?" he asked, wiping a stray tear away.

She nodded. "But Elaine has to say goodbye to him all over again."

"But won't she be happy?"

"Sure she will, but that doesn't make it any easier."

Bradley put his arms around her shoulders and led her to the stairs. "Come on, you need your sleep."

He stopped in front of her bedroom door. "Thank you for letting me help you," he said. "Not only was it an honor to help that young soldier, it helped me understand why what you do is so important."

He placed a kiss on her forehead. "Good night, Mary."

Chapter Thirty-Six

Christmas was one week away and there was no sign of Kevin Brady anywhere. "I think he's skipped the country," Mary said. "He's not coming to Freeport and we are not in danger."

"You don't know that for sure, Mary," Sean's voice flowed through the speaker phone into her office. "We still have a BOLO out for him throughout the Chicagoland area."

"Sean, even with your Be-On-the-Look-Out, we can't keep living in a state of alert," she argued. "Poor Bradley's been sleeping in my guest room for three weeks."

"Hey, wait," Bradley interrupted. "Don't pull me into this; I'm fine with the sleeping arrangements."

"Yeah, I'll just bet you are," Sean said.

"She makes breakfast for me every morning," Bradley said. "I don't think I'll ever leave."

"Listen, I can't put my life on hold any longer," she said. "My friends are getting tired of babysitting me and, quite frankly, I think this is all unnecessary at this point."

I am getting way too used to having Bradley around all the time, she wanted to scream. *My heart's in far more danger than my life ever was.*

Sean sighed. "Mary, we don't know where he is. It still might not be safe."

"Okay, how about a compromise," she said. "I get to go to my office and work, by myself. I get to do some Christmas shopping in town, by myself. And I get to sleep, by myself."

"She didn't mean that the way it sounded," Bradley interjected.

Mary blushed. "I mean, Bradley gets to sleep at his own house. But I will carry my revolver with me wherever I go. I will let someone, probably Bradley, know of my every move and I'll carry a walkie-talkie so I can have instant communication with whoever you want me to communicate with."

"Bradley, how do you feel about her plan?"

"Well, other than the fact I'm giving up breakfast and living with Mary," he grinned at her, "I think she's right. We've had no Brady sightings at all. All of the local law enforcement personnel have his photo, as do all of the hotels, motels and bed and breakfasts. He isn't going to stay in the Freeport area without someone seeing him and reporting it."

"I know you could both do whatever you want, without consulting me," Sean said. "But I appreciate you keeping me in the loop. You're probably right; Kevin Brady is far away from Illinois by now."

Sean's voice echoed from the speaker into the vacant space around Kevin Brady. He sat back and munched another French fry while he listened to the end of the conversation. "Well, Chief Alden, I'm not

236

going to be able to stay in the Freeport area without someone seeing me?" he taunted. "So much for your psychic ability."

He looked around the large empty building and smiled. He was sitting in the heart of downtown Freeport, in the old Rawleigh Complex, only four blocks away from Mary's office. The four-hundred-thousand-square-foot brownstone complex consisted of four large buildings that had once housed manufacturing, warehousing, laboratory, and office floor space for the production of infamous Rawleigh medical products.

Abandoned in 1988, the large structure sat unoccupied, like a ghost town waiting for new habitation. Its windows were broken, its brick façade cracked and its floors littered with the forgotten refuse of yesterday. Brochures touting wonder drugs like anti-pain oil, camphor balm, liniments, and cough syrup were still scattered on the floor. Chemical labs still held residues of past experiments. Conveyor systems still threaded their way through the buildings.

Although cold and drafty, the Rawleigh Building had been the perfect place to set up shop. The upper floors in the tallest building had windows that were still intact, yet were far enough up that any noise would be undetected. His generator not only provided heat, it allowed him to run the other electronic devices necessary to his plan.

The tap had been easy enough. Mary had left her office unused for several weeks. No one paid any attention to a service man making some upgrades to the lines behind the building. He looked at the monitor in front of him. The camera he installed right outside Mary's office allowed him to see whatever went on inside. He had to bide his time until just the right moment.

He opened the plastic container, dabbed his finger in the white powder and rubbed it on his gums. Sitting back, he smiled while the cocaine entered his system. He could feel the heat building between his legs while he watched Mary move around her office. He imagined what it was going to be like once he had her under his control. *Oh, yeah, she is going to enjoy what I have planned for her, but not nearly as much as I am going to enjoy it.*

Chapter Thirty-seven

"It's Tuesday," Mary said into the phone. "It's shop late 'til eight night, and it's three days until Christmas. Lots of people will be downtown. I'll be just fine."

"I don't feel good about this Mary," Bradley responded. "I have to go into Rockford for a meeting tonight and I won't be back until after ten."

"Bradley, I appreciate your concern, but I'm going to be fine. Kevin is not in Freeport. Sean called me this morning and said someone thought they saw him in L.A. He's a long way from here."

"Yeah, Sean called me too, but I still feel uneasy."

Mary smiled. "Your spidey-sense?"

He chuckled. "Yeah, my spidey-sense."

"I'll tell you what, I'll call Stanley, he's going to be downtown late anyway," she said. "And I'll have him walk me to my car. Okay?"

"Okay. Thanks for putting up with my worries."

"Hey, it's nice to be worried about," she said. "Have a good meeting."

As soon as she hung up, she placed the call to Stanley. "Hi, I need a favor," she said. "I need a walk to my car tonight, about eight-thirty. Would that work for you?"

"Sure, I'll be closing up here about that time," he said. "I like having a cute gal on my arm, even if it's only for half a block."

"Thanks, Bradley is still worried."

"He's a good man," Stanley said. "A girl could do a lot worse."

Mary sighed. "I know Stanley, but he is married."

"What kind of wife up and disappears on her husband for almost nine years, I ask you?"

"We don't know what the circumstances were," Mary said. "And, if Bradley loved her, she has to be pretty special."

"Okay, girlie, you've got a point," he said. "I'll give her the benefit of the doubt. So you want me to give our special knock?"

"We have a special knock?" Mary asked with a grin.

"Sure we do, two knocks, a pause and then two more knocks," he said.

"Oh...that secret knock," she said with a grin. "That'd be great. I'm going to close the blinds before it gets dark, so I'll know it's you."

"Alright, girlie, see you at eight-thirty."

"See you then, Stanley. And thanks!"

Several hours later, Stanley turned off the lights at Wagners' Office Supplies and walked over to the front door. He'd locked it after the last customer, so he could count the cash in the register and put together the deposit for the next day. He had just pulled the keys out of his pocket when he heard a noise in the office furniture section of the store. He glanced up to the clock, it was only eight-twenty-five, he still had a few minutes before he had to go next door and pick up Mary.

The glow from the streetlight was enough light for Stanley to make his way back through the store. He wondered if someone had left a fan running. Careless salespeople were always doing something like that. Did they think electricity was free?

He looked down the aisle that housed sample cubicles. Sure enough, at the end of the aisle was a fan running full force. He stepped into the aisle, shaking his head. Someone would be getting a talking to tomorrow morning.

The sharp pain to the back of his head barely registered before he fell unconscious to the floor. Kevin leaned down and picked up the keys Stanley had dropped. Whistling to himself, he wandered back to the front of the store. Things were going according to plan.

Two knocks, a pause and two more knocks. "I'll be right there, Stanley," Mary called, as she picked up her purse and computer case.

She clicked off the lights and stepped out the door, her back to the street as she inserted the key into the lock. "Hello, Mary," Kevin whispered, wrapping his arm around her waist and pulling her against him. "Sorry Stanley can't see you home. He's been detained."

She inhaled, ready to scream, when she felt the unmistakable pressure of the barrel of a gun pressed against her side. "Ah, Mary, you don't want to make a fuss, do you?" he whispered, his mouth next to her ear. "You don't want any of your friends to die, do you?"

She shook her head. "No, no need to hurt anyone," she said.

He laughed softly and kissed her on the neck. "Oh, Mary, so wise and so delicious, I am going to thoroughly enjoy you."

"Kevin, you know people are watching for you," she said. "You won't get away with this."

"Mary, Mary, such a clichéd statement. Of course I'm going to get away with it. I've been in your town for over a week. I've made plans. And once I drug you, you'll do anything I want you to do," he whispered into her ear. "My own personal plaything."

"I'd rather die," Mary spat.

He laughed softly. "Well, of course. I'll do that too."

Mary drove the four blocks to the Rawleigh Building, Kevin's gun trained on her. He had her park in one of the abandoned freight yards, and then he pulled her from the car. Most of the streetlamps around the vacant building had been broken by vandals, so they walked through shadows. Kevin held Mary around the waist, with his gun ever present in her side.

She knew she had to get away before he was able to inject her with drugs. As far as she was concerned, death was a far better alternative to the hell he was planning on putting her through.

He pulled her through a door in the old shipping area. "Welcome to my home," he said. "You can scream as loud as you'd like and no one can hear you. No GPS signals can be picked up in here. And in the time I've been here, no one has ventured even close to these buildings. It's our little paradise, Mary."

The walkie-talkie in Mary's purse beeped. "Mary, can you hear me?" Bradley's voice was muffled by the purse.

"Take it out," Kevin said, nudging her with the gun.

Mary pulled it out.

"Answer him."

"Hello, Bradley," she said, her voice shaking.

"Mary, what's wrong?"

Kevin grabbed the walkie-talkie from Mary's hand. "Well, hello there, Chief! Guess who?"

"Brady. You touch her and you will die."

Kevin laughed. "Wow! That was original. I'm not only going to touch her, I'm going to use her in every possible way I can, and there isn't a damn thing you can do about it. 'Bye for now, Chief. I've got a date with Mary."

He threw the walkie-talkie against the concrete floor and it shattered into tiny pieces. "Now, let's go up to the penthouse suite and get comfortable."

The inside of the building was dark, the few street lights barely penetrating the boarded windows. Mary waited for her eyes to adjust.

She could see the outline of a freight elevator in front of them. Kevin pulled her in that direction. If she could distract him, perhaps she could get away.

"Did you know it wasn't Bradley who could see the ghosts?" Mary said. "It was me. I could see them. I spoke with Jack. You killed your own partner."

Kevin shook his head. "He gave me no choice. He would have sent them home. He would have messed up the deal."

The freight elevator was an ancient behemoth from the early 1900s lacking the safety features in more modern equipment. "Watch your step," Kevin said, as he dragged Mary over the six-inch gap between the floor and the elevator. "I'd hate to lose you before we had a chance to get to know each other better."

Large metal gates slid from the top and the bottom and met in the middle with a clang. The elevator was lit by a single bulb hanging from a thick black wire, causing shadows to dance as the elevator moved, its mechanism creaking eerily as they ascended. The floor of the elevator was scattered with papers and broken sections of pallets.

"He's here, Kevin," Mary said. "Jack's here and wants to know why you killed him. He trusted you. He saved your life."

"You're lying," Kevin said, twisting her arm back behind her. "You're nothing but a lying bitch."

"Ask me a question only Jack would know and I'll prove it."

"I don't need to ask any questions. Jack's dead and he's gonna stay that way."

"He won't rest until his killer is brought to justice," she said. "He won't rest until they catch you. You can't run from a ghost, Kevin."

"Shut up!" Kevin screamed as he twisted her around and slapped her across the face. The impact sent her sprawling to the floor of the freight elevator. "Just shut up!"

Mary rolled to the side of the elevator and slid a pointed piece of wood from a broken pallet up her sleeve.

"Get up," Kevin demanded.

Mary quickly climbed to her feet. Kevin smiled. "That's more like it," he said. "I'll teach you to be obedient."

Like hell you will, Mary thought.

Chapter Thirty-eight

With his siren blaring, Bradley was driving west on Highway 20 as fast as safety would allow. He had notified all of the local law enforcement agencies that Kevin had abducted Mary. Pulling off the Highway, he careened onto Adams Street and headed toward downtown.

He was sure he heard an echo while Kevin was talking to him on the walkie-talkie, which meant they were indoors. Mary wasn't scheduled to leave her office until eight-thirty and he called her no later than eight-forty-five. In order to be indoors, they still had to be in the downtown area.

He drove past the Stephenson County Prison and continued to speed up the street. The radio on his dashboard was relaying the current information on the search. They had divided the downtown into quadrants and teams were going through buildings systematically. So far, no one had found anything bringing them any closer to finding Mary. He hoped to God Mary was somehow able to get away from Kevin before he drugged her.

The elevator stopped on the top floor of the building. Mary was surprised to see the glow of electronics coming from work tables set up near the windows. Kevin grabbed her arm and pulled her forward. "Welcome to our little getaway," he said.

"Get real, Kevin," she said. "You really think they aren't going to turn this town apart looking for me?"

"Babe, when I get through with you, you're going to go with me wherever I say," he said. "I just need to lay low long enough for the drugs to kick in. Then it's free sailing all the way."

Mary scanned the area. The windows were still intact, so the ambient light was greater here than downstairs. Although still shadowy, Mary could see the area around her. Most of the floor was open with four-foot diameter pillars scattered throughout the space. At either end of the floor were doors that led to offices. She could also see a staircase at the far corner of the room, but had no idea if the stairs were still intact.

Kevin still had her arm in his grasp as he pulled her toward his work area. "I think you'll like this," he said as he pulled her around the table.

Mary felt her blood run cold. Against one wall he had fashioned a pair of shackles that had been fastened to the concrete. "I thought this would keep you secure, yet handy," he said. "See, Mary, I've thought of everything."

Mary worked the piece of wood down into her palm. She turned to Kevin and smiled. "I didn't realize how resourceful you were," she said.

He loosened his grip and slid his hand up and down her arm. "I think you'll find I have many talents."

She whipped her arm around and stabbed the piece of wood into his throat. He screamed, releasing her arm, as he reached for the wood protruding from his neck.

Mary ran toward the stairs.

Kevin grabbed hold of the wood and pulled it out, blood pouring from the wound. "You're going to pay for this, bitch," he yelled, pointing his gun at her and shooting.

Mary heard the bullet ricochet off one of the large pillars near her head. She kept running, dodging back and forth between the pillars. She could hear his footsteps gaining on her. The beginning of the staircase was covered with debris, mostly plaster that had fallen from the ceiling. She glanced further down; the stairs disappeared into inky darkness. Another shot hit the wall near her. Her decision was made; she was going to take the stairs.

Clutching the handrail, she ran down the stairs as quickly as she could. Once she reached the first landing, she dashed to the wall side of the staircase, staying in the shadows as much as she could.

"Where are you, you bitch?" Kevin screamed, staring into the dark. "You won't get away from me."

Mary kept her hands clasped onto the rail; she couldn't see far enough in front of her to tell if the staircase was safe or had been removed. She didn't need to fall six stories down to a concrete floor. She could hear Kevin struggling down the stairs behind her. Then she saw the beam of his flashlight scouring the area. She dove down several steps to avoid being caught in its light but when she reached the landing between the fifth and fourth floor, she stepped into a hole where the landing should have been.

Mary struggled to grab onto something. Her hand brushed papers, cardboard and smooth concrete. She dug her fingernails into the concrete and scrambled with her arms and legs, but she was still slipping through the hole. Finally, at the edge of the hole she caught hold of a piece of exposed rebar and halted her descent.

She felt around with her feet for something to step on to get back up to the landing, but all she felt was air.

The flashlight beam danced along the wall of the fifth floor, Kevin was getting closer.

# # # #

Bradley continued up Adams, trying to decide where he should look first. His teams had searched the Masonic Temple and the Lindo Theater, two of the larger buildings in the downtown area. They had also gone through many of the older brownstones that had empty office space, but there were no signs of Mary.

Bradley passed the armory, but it was deserted and no cars were in the parking lot. That building was too secure; Kevin wouldn't have been able to get inside. He drove past the Freeport Area

Church Cooperative Building, but it was filled with people and he didn't think Kevin would risk going there. Finally, he entered the downtown area. He scanned the parking lots and alleys, hoping to see Mary's Roadster.

Where the hell would he take her?

Bradley slowed the cruiser and pulled over for a moment. He needed to think it through; he would just waste time if he reacted in a panic. *Kevin would have thought it out. He would have created a secure place to hold Mary. This was not a random act, Kevin was not impulsive, and his revenge was too important to him.*

Bradley ran his hand through his hair and took a deep breath.

But where the hell could he accomplish all that in the middle of downtown Freeport?

A shimmer of light caught his eye. He turned and saw it again. Someone was signaling him from the top of the Rawleigh Building. He tried to see if it was Mary, but could only see the flickering of the light. He whipped the cruiser back behind the building and stopped next to a loading dock. The entry where the door had once stood had been boarded over. Bradley pulled a "jaws of life" tool out of his trunk and climbed up on the dock. Sliding the tool between the building and the plywood, he quickly pulled the plywood away from the building far enough to slip in.

The flicker appeared again across the room. Bradley pulled his gun out of his holster and followed the light.

#

Mary could see the bottom of Kevin's legs on the staircase above her. She considered her options. She could stay where she was, hanging down a hole in the landing, and hope that Kevin wouldn't find her, or she could drop down and hope that the landing below was intact. And that she didn't break something during the fall.

If Kevin got hold of her again, she didn't think he'd give her another chance to escape. But if she broke her leg, could she still move enough to escape?

Kevin came closer.

Mary reached across the landing with one hand and grabbed hold of a packing box. She quietly slid it over and laid it on top of her head and shoulders. Perhaps the flashlight would glance over it and he'd miss her.

She heard him stop and could see the beam slowly scan the area. It stopped next to her.

"Well, little Mary has herself in quite a predicament," he said.

Mary's heart dropped. She heard him stepping down the final steps to the landing. "Don't worry, Mary, I'll take care of you," he laughed.

Suddenly Mary felt strong hands grab her legs from below. She released the rebar and allowed herself to fall. Bradley lowered her into his arms.

"Damn, you are going to be the death of me," he whispered, hugging her quickly and then placing her on the ground.

"How did you find me?" she asked.

"I saw your signal."

"What? I didn't signal…"

The beam from Kevin's flashlight shone through the hole in the landing. Bradley and Mary dropped back against the wall. "Mary," he called. "I'm coming down to get you."

"Let him come," Bradley murmured.

The debris rustled and Mary and Bradley watched as Kevin made his way down the steps. Halfway down, his gun barrel extended in front of him, Kevin stopped. "Who's there?"

Mary and Bradley exchanged confused glances.

"Who are you?" Kevin screamed. "Who the hell are you?"

Kevin turned and ran back up the stairs. "No, no, stay away."

Mary and Bradley followed at a careful distance. Kevin ran up the stairs like he was being chased. "Do you see anything?" Bradley asked.

Mary shook her head, then put her hand in Bradley's. "Do you?"

Bradley scanned the staircase. "No, nothing," he said. "Maybe it's the drugs."

They entered the eighth floor and watched Kevin dash across the room. "No," he screamed. "Stay away."

"Mary, stay here, by the stairs," Bradley said. "I'll circle around."

Then Mary saw her, the ghost she had seen at the hospital and hotel room. She was on the other side of the room, but she was just standing there, not following Kevin.

The sound of the freight elevator's descent rumbled throughout the building. Kevin turned and ran toward it.

"Kevin, freeze," Bradley yelled. "Police."

Kevin turned, his gun drawn and aimed at Bradley.

"No!" Mary screamed.

A light flickered across the room; its beam shone onto Kevin's face, blinding him.

Mary heard a shot. Then there was silence.

She looked across the room. The ghost smiled sadly and faded away.

Mary turned to where she had last seen Bradley. He was lying face-down on the ground near the work tables and Kevin was standing near the freight elevator shaft, gun in hand. "Bradley," Mary screamed.

Kevin turned and looked directly at her. He started to lift his gun in her direction, but stopped and stared down as blood blossomed on his chest. He dropped his arm and staggered backward. The doors of the freight elevator opened, but the elevator was on the bottom floor. Kevin toppled backward into the open shaft. Mary heard the crash when his body hit the ground.

Bradley stood up, brushing the debris from his clothes. "Well, that was close," he said, he looked over at Mary. "You okay?"

She nodded slowly as her legs gave out from underneath her and she slipped down to the floor.

Chapter Thirty-nine

"I want you to go to the Emergency Room," Bradley insisted, motioning the paramedics over to where he and Mary sat on the floor.

"I'm fine," she said. "I just need to make sure Stanley's okay, and then I need to sleep."

"You fainted right in front of me," Bradley argued.

"I thought you were dead," Mary argued back. "It was a little bit of a shock."

"Why in the world did you think I was dead?"

"Because you were lying on the floor," she said, "after I heard a shot."

Bradley paused for a moment. "Oh," he said. "I didn't think about that, sorry. It was a tactical move, to avoid getting shot. But I still think you need to be checked over."

She leaned forward and whispered in his ear, "Bradley, I really hate hospitals."

He sighed and turned back to the waiting paramedics. "It seems I'm wrong," he said. "Miss O'Reilly is perfectly fine.

"But you sit there quietly until I can help you down the stairs," he whispered to her. "Got it?"

She nodded. "Got it. Thanks."

Bradley walked over to a group standing by the freight elevator. A second set of paramedics at the bottom of the shaft had just zipped Kevin into a body bag and were getting ready to transport him to the morgue. "Make sure Sean O'Reilly, Special Victims Unit, Chicago Police Force gets a copy of the report," he said to an officer standing close by.

"Yes, sir."

"I want all this stuff tagged and moved to the evidence locker," he told one of his detectives. "There might be some evidence that will link him with some of the murders in Chicago."

Another officer came running over. "Bradley, I just got a call," he said. "They found Stanley in his store. He's got a lump on his head, but he's fine."

"Thanks, I'll let Mary know."

He walked back over to Mary who sat shivering on the floor. "Dammit, Mary, I'm sorry, I should have known you would have been cold," he said.

Mary shook her head. "I'm not cold," she stammered. "I just can't seem to stop shaking."

He sighed and scooped her up into his arms. "Come on, there's another freight elevator in the front of the building," he said. "I'm taking you home."

She laid her head on his shoulder. "What's wrong with me?"

"I'd make a wild guess and say shock," he said. "You've had a pretty frightening night."

She shuddered again. "I just couldn't let him drug me," she said. "I just couldn't let him touch me…"

He hugged her tighter, remembering the shackles he saw next to the work area. "Yeah, I know."

"Did you hear about Stanley?" she asked.

"Yeah, they found him in his store. He's got a bad bump on his head, but he's going to be fine. Sounds like he was madder than all get-out because he missed the excitement, though."

She laughed. "Sounds just like him."

The elevator stopped on the first floor and the gates opened. "We can pick your car up later," he said. "I'll drive you home."

He placed her in the cruiser, pulled a blanket from the back and tucked it firmly around her. "My purse, my briefcase," she protested mildly.

"My guys will get it for you," he said. "You won't need them tonight."

Bradley's phone rang as soon as he sat in his seat. He looked at the display. "It's Sean," he said. "I should talk to him."

Mary nodded and listened to Bradley's side of the conversation.

"Sean. Yeah, she's fine. Suffering from a little shock, but that's understandable. Yeah, she was amazing. He was in pretty bad shape before I got there."

He paused and listened for a moment.

"No, we're not going to the hospital, but I'll make sure she's okay. Yeah, he's filling a space at the morgue right now," Bradley looked over and saw the information register on Mary's face. He reached

257

over, took her hand in his and squeezed it softly. "If you want him, you can have him. I'll take care of the paperwork tomorrow."

He listened again.

"Hey, no need to thank me," he said, looking at Mary once again. "Like I told you before, I wouldn't think of doing anything else. Okay, I'll touch base with you tomorrow. Goodbye."

"So Kevin's dead," Mary said.

"Yeah, the paramedics believe he died on impact," Bradley said.

"I wonder what was chasing him," she mused. "I couldn't see anything."

"And something started the freight elevator before he came near it," Bradley said.

"I saw Jack there earlier. He was in the freight elevator with us. He was pretty angry about how Kevin was treating me."

Bradley skimmed his hand over her cheek, her bruises now showing more clearly under the street lights of the city. "I understand how he feels."

"I don't know how I feel," Mary said. "It's almost too much to take in. He used to be my brother's friend and now…"

"Now he let drugs turn him into a different person," Bradley said. "The Kevin that died tonight was not your friend. That Kevin died a long time ago."

Mary nodded. "You're right. It's just so sad."

Bradley pulled the cruiser to the curb in front of her house. "Stay seated," he said, and walked over to her door and helped her out. "How are you doing?"

She stepped out of the car and, although a little shaky, she felt like she could walk on her own. "I'm good," she said. "But don't go too far."

"Don't worry, I'm not going anywhere," he said, pulling the blanket tight, wrapping his arm around her and walking her to the door.

He led her upstairs to her bedroom. "I want you to take a hot shower and dress in something warm," he ordered. "Did you eat dinner?"

She shook her head. "No, but really, I don't think I could eat anything."

"Okay, shower, then come downstairs."

Bradley was right, the hot shower really helped revive her. Dressed in sweats and thick cotton socks, she felt much better. She came down the stairs to find the downstairs dark.

"Bradley?" she called, slightly panicked.

"Mary," he said, hurrying to her side. "Sorry, I wasn't quite ready for you."

He led her to the couch and wrapped a soft quilt around her, and then he turned on the Christmas tree and let the lights sparkle around the room. He clicked on the CD player and soft Christmas music filled the room.

She felt her whole body relax. He pulled a TV tray in front of the couch.

"Be right back," he said.

Moments later there were two cups of herbal tea and a plate of Christmas cookies on the tray. "Who can turn down Christmas cookies?" he asked.

She smiled up at him. "Thank you. This is exactly what I needed."

He sat down next to her, pulled her into his arms and laid his cheek on the top of her head. He exhaled softly. "Thank you. This is exactly what *I* needed."

Chapter Forty

The next day, Bradley and Mary went to see Stanley in the hospital. "I see you got enough connections so you don't have to stay in this god-forsaken place," Stanley growled.

Mary smiled. "I didn't get knocked over the head," she said. "They were worried about a concussion."

Bradley shook his head. "No, from what I heard, they just wanted to make him miserable," he said. "The doc said his head was too hard to be in any danger."

Stanley chuckled. "That's what I thought."

"When can you go home?" Mary asked.

"I'll be out of here by noon," he said. "It's the day before Christmas Eve; I've got things to do."

Mary leaned over and pressed a kiss on the top of Stanley's head. "Thank you for being there for me. I'm sorry…"

Stanley caught her hand in his. "Listen, girlie, this bump on my head don't have nothing to do with you. I'm embarrassed that I let that jackass get the best of me. I should have known better."

Bradley nodded. "Yes, you of all people should have known better."

"Bradley!' Mary chided. "That wasn't nice."

Stanley chuckled. "Not as slow as I thought you were."

Bradley smiled. "No, indeed," he replied.

"What's going on?" Mary asked.

"I had a conversation with Sean this morning about why his local informant wasn't very helpful last night," Bradley said. "Seems his informant let some jackass get the best of him."

"Stanley?" Mary asked, astonished. "But…"

"Sean? Sean who?" Stanley interrupted. "I understand a knock on the head can cause amnesia. I think I probably have the early signs of amnesia."

"Stanley," Mary said, "don't you try to pull that on me."

Stanley leaned back on his pillow. "Can't a man get any rest around here?" he asked. "I thought this place was supposed to be a hospital, not Grand Central Station."

Bradley laughed out loud. "Come on, Mary," he said. "We'd better let Stanley get his strength back. I have a feeling he's going to need it."

They heard Stanley chuckling to himself as they walked out of his room.

Later that evening, Mary and Bradley walked from his car down a quiet street in the Center School neighborhood. The houses were all decorated for the season, lights shining against the snow, glowing in the dark night. Mary wrapped her arm around Bradley's and took a deep breath. "It smells like Christmas," she said, and then she looked around. "Someone's baking cookies."

262

"I wonder if there is a law on the books where it's legal for the police chief to confiscate cookies?" he asked.

She grinned. "Hmmm, that's certainly an ordinance that ought to be on the books. Of course, we'll end up with a police chief the size of Boss Hogg."

"Wow, from Andy Taylor to Boss Hogg," Bradley said, shaking his head. "I see I've come down in your estimation."

"Actually, it was Barney Fife to Boss Hogg," she quipped. "So, really, if you measure by pounds, you've actually increased in my opinion."

"Oh, thanks a lot."

"My pleasure."

They reached the tenth house of the block and climbed up the stairs.

"I'm excited to see him again," Mary said.

Bradley nodded. "Yes, me too," he said.

He reached over her shoulder and rang the doorbell. A young woman answered the door. "You must be Mary O'Reilly, and you're Chief Alden," she said. "I'm Patrice Marcum. Please come in."

The modest house was clean and tidy and decorated for the holiday season with a tiny tree sitting in a playpen. The woman met Mary's gaze and laughed. "We had to put it in there to protect it," she said. "Jeremy scoots all over the place now."

Mary grinned. "Well, that's brilliant."

She looked around the room and saw Joey sitting next to the fireplace, with a big dog next to him. He smiled at her and waved.

Then she saw the man sitting in the recliner in the corner of the room. "Hello. I'm Mel Marcum," he said, extending his hand toward them. "Please excuse me, I can't quite walk yet. But the doctors think I'll be up and walking in no time at all."

Mary took his hand. "That's wonderful," she said.

"I can't begin to thank you for what you did for us," Patrice said. "If you hadn't found him, and then if you hadn't jumped in the river."

"We were happy to do it," Bradley said. "We're just glad it turned out the way it did."

"I never thought I'd be happy again," Patrice said. "Then, when something like this happens, it really gives you a different perspective on life."

Jeremy was on a blanket near the Christmas tree; he saw Bradley and lifted his arms up toward him. Bradley bent down and picked him up. "Hey, big fella, you've gained at least thirty pounds since the last time I saw you."

Mary kissed Jeremy on the cheek. "He looks so happy and healthy. Did he suffer any adverse reactions?"

Patrice shook her head. "No, the doctors said that everything is fine. There is one odd thing he does now, that he never did before," she said.

"What's that?" Bradley asked.

"He'll be in his crib and he'll stand up and laugh and wave, like someone was there," she said. "And I could swear he's tried to say doggie. But we don't have a dog."

"Funny thing is," Mel chimed in. "Sometimes I think I can smell a dog."

"Imagine that," Bradley said, winking at Mary.

"You know, they say that when people have a near death experience, it brings them closer to the other side," Mary said. "Perhaps he's just seeing an angel."

Patrice nodded, her eyes filling with tears. "Our son, Joey, died just before Jeremy was born," she said. "I've always felt that he was still here. That he was watching out for Jeremy. Do you think I'm crazy?"

Mary gave Patrice a hug. "No, I think you're a very wise woman."

Patrice walked over to the fireplace and took down a photo. There was Joey with his familiar grin. "What a wonderful smile," Mary said.

Then she saw the leather sack in the corner of the photo. "What's that?"

"Joey collected marbles," Mel said. "They were like treasure to him. We keep the bag of marbles on the hearth too, just to keep a piece of Joey with us always."

Mary looked over and saw the leather sack sitting in the corner of mantle. "That's very nice," she said.

265

"Except the cat's eye," Patrice said, running her hand over the photo frame. "We kept all the marbles but the cat's eye. It was his very favorite."

"Yeah, we placed it in his hand when he was buried," Mel said, tears filling his eyes. "We figured that he'd want it with him."

They visited for another thirty minutes, Jeremy entertaining them all, but then it was time for Mary and Bradley to leave.

"Excuse me," Mary said. "May I use your bathroom before we go?"

"Oh, certainly," Patrice said. "It's right down the hall to your left."

Mary motioned to Joey and they walked to the bathroom together.

"How are you doing?" she asked, after she closed the door.

"It's great at my house now," he said. "My dad's back, Jeremy's back and my mom's happy again. Thank you, Mary."

"Joey, it was my pleasure," she said. "You are the greatest young man I have ever met. It was a pleasure working a case with you."

He grinned up at her.

"But I have a problem and I need your help," she said.

Joey looked serious. "What do you need?"

Mary shook her head. "I can't keep my dog," she said. "I just work too many hours. I need to find another home for him."

"Really, you don't want Chief?"

Mary grinned. "Chief? That's what you named him? Won't Bradley be pleased!"

Joey nodded. "Yeah, it was either Chief or Hero, but those two words mean pretty much the same thing to me."

"You're right," she said. "They do mean the same thing. I'm sure Bradley will be honored. So, can you keep him for me?"

Joey grinned. "That's the best Christmas present ever," he said.

"I'm sure Chief will feel the same way."

"I have a present for you," Joey said. "But it's not ready yet. So, I'll get it to you later, okay?"

"Okay, there's still two more days until Christmas," Mary said. "You've got plenty of time."

"Mary, is it okay if I love you?" Joey asked.

Tears filled Mary's eyes and she laid her hand over her lips for a moment. "That would work just perfectly, Joey, because I love you too."

Chapter Forty-one

The doorbell rang at the same time the oven timer went off. "Bradley will you answer the door?" Mary called, as she pulled the appetizers out of the oven.

Bradley walked across the room and pulled open the front door. Linda Lincoln walked in. "Hi Linda," Bradley said. "Merry Christmas Eve. Let me help you with your coat."

"Thanks Bradley, good to see you," she said, slipping out of her coat. "Isn't it nice of Mary to have this little party for us single folks on Christmas Eve?"

Bradley hung the coat in the closet. "Yeah, it really is. Come on in to the kitchen," he said. "That's where we're hanging out, because that's where the food is."

Laughing, they walked together into the kitchen. Mary was placing the appetizers on a tray and another man was sitting at the kitchen counter. "Linda, do you know Bob Sterling?" Bradley asked.

"Bob, how are you?" Linda asked. "Isn't that funny, Mary and I were just discussing you last week. It's so good to see you."

Bob smiled back. "It's great to see you too, Linda, you look wonderful."

268

"Let's all go into the front room," Mary suggested. "I'll bring the food. Bradley, can you get the eggnog?"

They sat around the coffee table, Mary and Bradley on the couch and Linda and Bob on the recliners across from them. They chatted about small town politics and shared friendly gossip for thirty minutes as they ate the appetizers and drank eggnog. Finally Mary stood up, walked to the fireplace and pulled down a couple of letters from the mantle.

"I have to tell you this amazing story I learned last week," she said. "I think you'll both find it very interesting. I met Elaine Kenney last week, she was Patrick Kenney's mother," she began. "You both remember Patrick, don't you?"

They nodded.

"Well, she pulled out some of Patrick's things to look through and we found an old cigar box filled with letters."

At the mention of the letters, Bob stiffened slightly.

"There were two piles of bound letters and a couple of loose ones at the bottom of the box. One pile of bound letters was those he had received from home. Linda, he had your letters in that group. And then...here's the interesting part, the other pile was filled with love letters he had sent you, Linda. I thought it was a little strange he would make a long-hand copy of his letters, but it was also kind of sweet."

"I suppose so," Linda said.

269

"Then his mother looked at one of the letters and realized it wasn't Patrick's handwriting."

"What?" Linda asked.

"And when we looked at the two loose letters in the bottom of the box, we saw a completed letter in the strange handwriting and a half-copied letter in Patrick's own hand."

Linda shook her head. "Why would he do something like that? Was someone else writing his letters to me?"

"You know, it's getting late, perhaps we ought to continue this story some other time," Bob said.

"Come on, Bob, the story's just getting to the interesting part," Bradley said. "Mary, tell them what else you found."

"Well, first, I have to add this to the story, which again, was so interesting to me," Mary said. "The same day I met with Patrick's mother, Linda came here for lunch. Do you remember Linda?"

Linda nodded.

"And she said the most interesting thing," Mary said. "I hope you don't mind if I share it."

"Well, actually, Mary…" Linda began.

"Linda said that she really wasn't in love with Patrick before he left," Mary interrupted. "She didn't really start falling in love with him until she started receiving his letters. She told me the writer of those letters was the man she fell in love with. Isn't that interesting, Bob?"

Bob sat back in his chair and a smile spread across his face. "Yes, that is very interesting, Mary."

"So, getting back to the original story," Mary said. "We also found a note in the bottom of the cigar box. A note from Patrick. Perhaps he felt something was going to happen to him, or perhaps he just wanted to clear his conscience. He wrote that, while he cared for Linda, he knew he wasn't in love with her. There was another man stationed with him, a man Patrick discovered adored Linda with all his heart. But because Patrick was going with her, he sat back and wrote letters to her that he never mailed and knew she would never see. Patrick found the letters and thought it would be a great joke to copy them and send them to Linda as if he had written them."

Linda glanced at Bob, and then quickly turned away.

"When his friend found out, he was angry and embarrassed. He didn't want to be a laughing stock and he didn't want to play games with Linda's feelings. Patrick could tell Linda really liked the letters and the person who had written them. So, he was going to write Linda and tell her the truth. Unfortunately, he died before he could tell her."

"The young man, his friend, who had loved Linda so much, was caught. He couldn't write her and tell her the truth. He couldn't betray the memory of his friend. So he finished his time in Vietnam and hurried home, back to the woman he loved."

271

"But she had already married someone else," Linda said. "And she didn't know the one true love of her life was still alive."

"I didn't know how to tell you," Bob said softly.

"Bradley, would you help me with something in the kitchen?" Mary said.

Bradley nodded. "Yeah, I'd be happy to help."

Mary and Bradley left the front room to leave Linda and Bob alone.

"The letters were beautiful," Linda said. "I still have them."

"I meant every word I wrote," Bob confessed.

"Where's the mistletoe when we need it?" Bradley whispered to Mary, sneaking a peek from the kitchen.

"Shhhh," Mary said with a grin.

"Mary," Linda called from the front room, "Bob and I are...we have to go. We hope you'll understand."

The front door opened and then closed. "I sure hope they remembered their coats," she said.

"I don't think they'll notice the cold," Bradley said.

"I like playing Cupid," Mary said.

"Yeah, it's a lot safer than falling in love yourself."

Chapter Forty-two

The log in the fire snapped loudly in the ensuing silence. Mary didn't know what to say. Christmas music played softly and the coals in the fireplace glowed, casting a warm hue to the room. The lights on the tree sparkled in the darkened room.

"They looked happy," Mary said finally, walking into the front room to pick up the plates and cups. "There's nothing like a happy ending."

Bradley nodded. "Yeah, they waited a long time for love."

She looked at him from across the room. "Sometimes love is worth waiting for."

"Mary…" he started.

She quickly moved past him into the kitchen. "How about a little more eggnog?" she asked, hurrying to the counter before she did something stupid.

Okay, more stupid, she chided herself. *Sometime love's worth waiting for…melodramatic much?*

"Mary," Bradley gently took hold of her arm to stop her. "We really need to talk."

She didn't turn around. She didn't want to see the look of kindness, or worse, pity, in his eyes. She searched for anywhere else to look when she spied the two objects on her counter.

"What's that?" she asked, stepping forward.

He released her arm and followed her. There were two envelopes on the counter. One had a large lump in it; the other was just a flat envelope.

The envelope with the lump had "Mary" printed in block letters. She opened it up and pulled out a letter crafted of construction paper and something wrapped in tissue paper. "It's from Joey," she said.

"Read it," Bradley encouraged.

"Merry Christmas," she read. "Thank you for saving Jeremy. I will always be your friend. This for you. I hope you like it. Love, Joey"

She didn't care about the tears that fell; she unwrapped the paper and found a large cat's eye marble nestled inside. "It was his favorite marble," she whispered, turning her face up to Bradley's.

He cupped her chin and gently wiped away her tears with his thumb. "My turn."

He opened the letter and read, "Dear Chief Alden, I know I kind of got in the way the last time. Maybe this time you can do it right. Look up! Love, Joey."

They both looked up and saw a bundle of mistletoe hanging from the ceiling. Bradley shook his head slowly and then looked down at Mary's upturned face. "He's right," he said softly. "I really need to do it better this time."

He slid his hand along her cheek and buried his fingers in her hair. Then he tenderly caressed her face with his other hand. "Mary."

He lowered his face and brushed his lips against hers once and then once more. He felt her body relax. Then, with a soft sigh, he crushed his lips to hers and pulled her tightly into his arms. Mary melted against him, joy building in her heart and exploding throughout her body. She slipped her hands into his hair, pulling him closer. "Oh, Bradley," she whispered.

He rained light kisses over her face and then onto her neck. She trembled in his arms. He moved back to her lips, parting them and tasting her sweet mouth. Mary shuddered, every nerve on edge, her body pulsing with need. Then suddenly, he was just holding her, wrapping her in his arms, his cheek resting on the top of her head. His breathing was rushed and his body tense. But his hands were gentle as he slid them slowly up and down her back. Finally, with the passion banked, he pulled away slightly and looked into her eyes. "Mary," he whispered, "I love you."

She smiled back at him, tears in her eyes. "I love you, too."

He pulled her back into his arms and held her. "I still...I still need to work some things out," he said. "But I can't hide what I feel for you anymore."

She lifted her head and kissed him softly on the lips. "I can wait," she said. "I feel like I've been waiting for you all my life."

He laid his forehead on hers. "I want to be sure we do this right," he said. "So I need to leave now, before I can't. Does that make any sense?"

She smiled. "Merry Christmas, Bradley. Stop by tomorrow for another round of mistletoe."

He kissed her on the tip of her nose. "Merry Christmas, Mary. I can't wait."

She walked him to the front room and they kissed. He took his coat out of the closet and they kissed. She walked him to the front door and they kissed again. He cupped her chin in his hand. "Don't forget...I love you," he said, kissing her once more before he slipped outside.

Mary turned the lock and leaned back against the door. *Miracles do happen!*

Chapter Forty-three

Mary stood in her darkened bedroom, staring out the window into the night sky. She was wrapped in her favorite terry bath robe and thick cotton socks. "I really can't stay, but baby it's cold outside," she sang with a giggle. *How could this day be any better?*

A lone star came out from behind the cloud cover and sparkled above the city. *My very own Christmas star,* Mary thought, hugging herself. *My very own fairytale come true.*

Suddenly she felt the hairs on the back of her neck raise and knew she was no longer alone. She turned around to see a dimly illuminated figure standing on the other side of her bed. She reached slowly for the bedside lamp and turned it on.

The same ghost she'd seen in the hospital, in their hotel room and finally, at the Rawleigh Building, stood before her.

"Thank you," Mary said. "I really didn't get a chance to say that earlier. You saved our lives."

The ghost smiled sadly and nodded.

"I want to help you," Mary said. "Would you like me to help you move on?"

The ghost nodded again.

"What's your name?"

The ghost sighed. "I'm Jeannine Alden, Bradley's wife."

About the author:

Terri Reid lives near Freeport, the home of the Mary O'Reilly Mystery Series, and loves a good ghost story. She lives in a hundred-year-old farmhouse complete with its own ghost. She loves hearing from her readers at author@terrireid.com.

Books by Terri Reid:

Loose Ends – A Mary O'Reilly Paranormal Mystery (Book One)

Good Tidings – A Mary O'Reilly Paranormal Mystery (Book Two)

Never Forgotten – A Mary O'Reilly Paranormal Mystery (Book Three)

Final Call – A Mary O'Reilly Paranormal Mystery (Book Four)

Darkness Exposed – A Mary O'Reilly Paranormal Mystery (Book Five)

Natural Reaction – A Mary O'Reilly Paranormal Mystery (Book Six)

Secret Hollows – A Mary O'Reilly Paranormal Mystery (Book Seven)

Broken Promises – A Mary O'Reilly Paranormal Mystery (Book Eight)

Twisted Paths – A Mary O'Reilly Paranormal Mystery (Book Nine)

Veiled Passages – A Mary O'Reilly Paranormal Mystery (Book Ten)

Bumpy Roads – A Mary O'Reilly Paranormal Mystery (Book Eleven)

The Ghosts Of New Orleans – A Paranormal Research and Containment Division (PRCD) Case File